Billionaire Unchallenged

THE BILLIONAIRE'S OBESSION
Carter

J. S. SCOTT

Contents

Chapter 1

Brynn

I *feel like I've spent every one of my twenty-nine years on this earth completely deprived of sweets!*

Regretfully, I shook my head at the tuxedo-clad waiter, and then watched him walk away with his tray of mouthwatering pastries. I'd already wasted my allowed calories for the day on alcohol, so I couldn't give in to the temptation to sample one of the carb-laden sweets, too.

"Well done, Brynn," my friend Laura remarked wryly from her seat beside me at the small table. "I'm not sure I have as much restraint as you do anymore, but then, I don't have to try to shove this curvy body into a size four anymore."

I smiled at Laura. "I don't either," I reminded her. "And I noticed that you didn't exactly help yourself to any, either."

At the age of twenty-nine, I still had an active modeling career, but Laura and I had made a pact years ago that we were going to be healthy, and prevent each other from being dangerously thin just so we could keep our careers as models. We'd bonded over that promise, a vow that had probably saved both our sanities and our health in an industry that was weight and size obsessed.

"I have a shoot next month," she said wistfully. "I might be a plus size model, but I still have to fit into the jeans."

"You look gorgeous," I answered emphatically. My friend was beautifully curvy, and drop-dead beautiful.

For years, Laura and I had fought for body diversity in modeling, and it had been a long, difficult road. Sure, the industry had started to use some models who represented a healthy, realistic lifestyle, but it wasn't enough.

Until the fashion industry got real and stopped considering a size twelve as plus size, there was *way* too far to go.

I was a straight size model, but only barely. I was a solid size six, and I was healthy. Years ago, I'd starved myself to fit into the size two or size four that clothing designers wanted me to model. But once Laura and I had hooked up and decided we'd rather be out of the profession than destroying our bodies for a lifetime, my mindset had changed. We'd both known we were on a dangerous downhill slide, mentally and physically. So we'd fought for body diversity because we'd already had a name in our profession.

Honestly, we were still fighting.

But we'd both reached the top of our game at sizes that were healthy for us. So I saw that as a small win.

Unfortunately, that didn't mean that I could eat whatever I wanted.

I loved sweets, but my ass *did not.*

Even though we'd made a promise to stop starving ourselves years ago, Laura and I were still supermodels, and that meant we had to eat well, work out, get plenty of sleep, and stay healthy.

"But I'm thirty-three," Laura finally said wistfully. "Other than a few lucrative gigs, my career is pretty much over."

I snorted. "Only because you want it to be," I said.

There was no reason in hell that she couldn't keep modeling. She'd *chosen* to slow down and be picky about what jobs she accepted, just like I had.

She shrugged. "I'm tired of globetrotting. And I've been happier since we started the Perfect Harmony clothing line."

Really, I'd been more content myself since I'd relocated to Seattle a year ago, too, following Laura so we could pursue our own clothing company, a line that was deeply personal because we felt that we represented women of all shapes, colors, and sizes.

We'd opened a small boutique on Fourth Avenue downtown, and I spent the majority of my time designing a line of clothing with Laura that we both loved.

I fit better in Seattle than I ever had in New York City. Not that the pace was that much slower, but the vibe in Seattle was...different. And our Perfect Harmony styles were so suited to this city.

The brand was all about personal style rather than fashion, and I loved every single creation. Laura and I had wanted comfortable, but stylish. Functional and easy to clean. Things that are definitely never considered in high fashion.

"Do you think we've stayed long enough?" Laura asked hopefully.

I laughed. Laura and I had come to the fundraiser cocktail party only because we both believed in the cause—domestic abuse. But I had to admit it was pretty much a sleeper.

As I surveyed the room, I spied plenty of older men in tuxedos, but they all looked like they were talking business, and their wives were standing dutifully at their sides.

"I already wrote my check, so I think we can get out of here pretty soon," I replied. My main goal had been to donate. It didn't matter whether I stayed at the venue or not.

I had nothing against a good party, but I was nursing the second drink I'd ordered because I couldn't have another one.

"I wrote mine, too," Laura said happily.

I surveyed the crowd again, noticing that most of the people hadn't really moved from their positions during the last hour we'd been at the fundraiser. Everybody was still chatting in small groups, or at tables like the one Laura and I were occupying.

I'd so rather be home working on my latest design for a handbag than hanging out at this party.

Note to self: *Skip the cocktail fundraisers and just mail the check.*
I was just about to tell Laura that we could leave when I spied a familiar face.

I wasn't actually acquainted with the guy I was currently staring at, but I knew exactly who he was. "That's Carter Lawson," I informed my friend. "And I'm pretty sure that the big guy beside him is the oldest Lawson brother, Mason."

I'd seen Carter Lawson's picture plenty of times. The gossip magazines loved him. His brothers Mason and Jett? Not so much. The youngest and oldest Lawson brothers seemed to stay out of the spotlight as much as possible. But Carter was the marketing genius behind the mega successful technology company, and his brothers were more hands-on with the majority of the innovative products that Lawson seemed to be cranking out at a speed that was almost scary.

"He's hot," Laura said with awe in her tone.

There was no denying that Carter Lawson was attractive. Okay, maybe *more* than a little attractive. He was in-your-face gorgeous. And seeing as I was five foot nine, I could appreciate the fact that he was tall. Really tall. The only male near him who topped his height was the guy built like a bulldozer next to him. His brother Mason. "I agree," I finally answered. "Carter is definitely hot."

"I wasn't talking about Carter," Laura said. "I was talking about his brother."

I eyed the man next to the world's perfect specimen of manhood to check out his sibling. Mason was ruggedly handsome, and the guy was a good two inches taller than Carter. He was broad, with massive shoulders, but he didn't look like he had spare flesh on his body. He was just…ripped.

"He's attractive," I conceded.

"He's a lot more than just attractive," she answered, not taking her eyes off Mason.

"I think we're staring," I told her.

"I doubt they'll notice. They seem to be in a serious conversation."

Laura was right. Carter and his older brother weren't at the event to have fun. Their expressions were stoic as they talked to two older men. I had a feeling the night was all business for them.

I felt a tingle go through my spine, and then an uncomfortable jolt directly between my thighs. It wasn't a sensation I was accustomed to, so it caught me by surprise.

I've never met him, but I'm attracted to him. How weird is that?

Then again, what woman wouldn't want to drag Carter Lawson to the nearest bed?

He put his hand in his pocket, looking as relaxed as he would be at home watching a ball game. Formal wear apparently loved him. But it wasn't just his physical appearance that wouldn't let me stop watching him. There was something else.

Carter Lawson was magnetic, sophisticated, and appeared to be the master of his world, and I had to wonder whether anybody else could tell that most of what he presented was a façade. I was fascinated because I was, for some reason, convinced that it was all an act. Maybe because so much of my own public persona was a lie, I could recognize another fraudster.

I have vulnerabilities, even though I present a confident exterior. And so does he.

Not that anybody ever saw those weaknesses. And I was fairly certain nobody saw Carter Lawson's, either.

I was startled as he suddenly turned his gaze in my direction, catching my eyes and pinning me to my chair like I was a bug in a science experiment.

It wasn't comfortable.

In fact, it was decidedly unnerving to be the subject of his intense gaze.

But I still couldn't break from his gaze.

He looked at me like he could see into my soul. I wasn't sure whether I was creeped out or mesmerized that he seemed to see the real me when nobody else did.

He recognizes somebody like him.

In an instant, I could sense how powerful he was, yet still realize that he was somewhat of a fraud.

A grin slowly formed on his sensual lips. Not a huge smile, but the kind of sexy expression a man has right before he takes a woman to bed and completely rocks her world.

"Brynn Davis and Laura Hastings? Oh, my God. I'm so excited that you're here!" I heard a high-pitched voice squeal as my eyes were still locked on Carter Lawson.

I ignored it because I couldn't seem to look away from the man whose eyes were stripping me bare.

My heart was galloping, and every nerve ending in my body was alive.

I was entranced.

I was captivated.

And I didn't want to break the connection, even though it was unsettling.

"That's us," Laura answered warmly right before she put her elbow into my arm to get my attention.

It was almost painful when I had to tear my eyes away from Carter's. His look was a challenge, and I wanted to figure out what he was daring me to do. But I looked away to acknowledge the newcomer beside the table because it was the polite thing to do.

I had a public persona that I was well-trained to pay attention to whenever I wasn't alone, whether people recognized me or not.

The young woman sat down in the chair next to me. "I'm Stephanie. I'm so excited. I didn't want to interrupt, but I just had to tell you that I love your positive body image blog."

The younger woman was pretty, and she was probably a decade younger than I was. "Thank you for following it," I said with genuine gratefulness.

Social media and online presence were critical for a model. Laura and I had millions of women who followed our blog and social media, and I was appreciative to every one of them who did.

They'd helped get me to where I was right now.

"It makes my bad days better," she said earnestly. "I guess it reminds me that it's okay to be different."

And *that* was exactly why Laura and I were out there every day. We'd been suckered into a world where perfect was determined by a designer who wouldn't fit into her own clothing.

Laura and I wanted women to realize that it was okay to love themselves, even if they didn't fit into some kind of mold other people expected.

Stephanie wasn't really overweight, but I'd discovered that most women who had a tendency to beat themselves up over their body type were often times just an average-size female. In a world that demanded perfection, it was so damn easy to find fault when there was none.

I nodded. "Good. That's why Laura and I blog."

We both wrote posts on the Perfect Harmony blog, and tried to get women to just accept who they were instead of comparing themselves to others.

"You're awesome," Stephanie stated emphatically.

I smiled at her. I'd gotten rid of my inability to deal with compliments years ago, or at least my brand had.

Now that Stephanie had come over to our table, we started to get more women flocking over to chat.

I was pretty certain her piercing scream had drawn the attention of the other females in the large room.

Not that I minded, especially at a public event. Laura and I couldn't have made millions of dollars without the people who like our work. And that money had given me a freedom that I was pretty damn grateful to have.

We chatted a lot about our blog, something Laura and I were passionate about, and about some of the events that were coming up in the next few months.

Laura whipped her phone out, and I followed suit, showing the women gathered around the table some of our pieces of clothing in our store.

"Oh, my God, I love that!" A chorus of approving voices surrounded us as we flipped through some of our outfits, and plenty of them vowed to hit our store the next day.

Mission accomplished.

Laura and I were both good at self-promotion. We'd always had to be.

I heaved a sigh of relief when, an hour later, the crowd around us had dissipated, and my friend and I could gracefully depart.

I glanced one more time at the gloriously gorgeous Carter Lawson.

I might be fascinated by him, but he's dangerous.

With those cautionary words ringing in my head, I hurried to get ready to leave with Laura. I'd learned to listen to my instincts, and I wasn't about to abandon them now.

Chapter 2

Carter

"That went well," I drawled to my brother, Mason, as the two men we'd been talking to the entire time we'd been at the fundraiser got into their car and drove away.

I stopped myself from tugging at the neck of my tuxedo shirt because of the Seattle humidity.

I was used to forcing myself to *never* look like I was uncomfortable.

But hell, it *was* summer, and although I enjoyed the mild winters, sometimes getting into a tux during the annoyingly humid and warm months was a necessity. I just made it a point to stay in air-conditioning.

But if I thought *I* was uncomfortable, Mason looked a hell of a lot worse. He ran a hand through his slightly damp hair, and then loosened his collar.

"I would have been happier if they'd left an hour ago," my brother grumbled. "Or we should have stayed inside. It's hotter than hell out here." He hesitated before he asked, "Do you think they'll sell?"

I shrugged. "I have no idea. But trying to get them to trust us is worth sweating our balls off."

Mason shot me an irritated look. "I doubt that. It's not like we *need* to acquire their company."

Maybe not. But Lawson Technologies was into world domination. So buying out a company that was competition and currently floundering was a goal we needed to make happen. "Perhaps it's not necessary," I agreed. "But you can't deny you'd like to absorb them."

"Because they've been a pain in my ass for years," Mason answered. "Anything we develop, they do the same."

"Not for long," I predicted. "Their financial situation is a mess. They have no choice but to sell."

"We'll see," Mason snapped irritably as he headed inside.

I followed, smirking because my brother's forehead was beaded with sweat.

Mason wasn't accustomed to getting out of the office much. Yeah, he did a lot of traveling, but it was all for business, and mostly to and from our offices around the world. But all that was accomplished in his private luxury jet that definitely had climate control.

Not that he was out of shape. He had private gyms everywhere, and my older brother was nothing if not disciplined.

Every single thing he did revolved around our giant tech company. I was pretty sure he ate, breathed, and slept Lawson Tech.

To be honest, I was starting to think Mason didn't even get laid. I wasn't sure when he'd find the time for it.

As we re-entered the venue, my eyes were automatically drawn to the table where I'd seen a woman I wanted to get into my bed. Strangely, I breathed a sigh of relief when I noticed that she and her friend were still there, but the crowd around them that had blocked my view of the stunning female was starting to disappear.

Mason stopped at the bar to get a drink, and I ordered one of my own.

I was surprised that my older brother's gaze was focused on the same place as mine was as I absently took my tumbler from the bartender.

"You interested?" I asked, my voice harsher than it should have been.

So what if he is? It's not like I get possessive over a female. Mason probably needs the distraction more than I do.

For some unknown reason, my mind screamed in protest at the thought of Mason taking the dark-haired seductress to his bed.

"She's gorgeous," Mason admitted, seemingly reluctant to say that he found a woman attractive. "She looks like a damn angel."

"The brunette?" I asked, startled. The woman looked more like the devil's creation to tempt a man until he went insane.

But I sure as hell wouldn't call her an angel.

She was sensual.

She was seductive.

And she looked at me like she could see straight through me—which she definitely didn't. If she could, she'd be running.

Her dark hair had a touch of cinnamon that made me want to plunge my hands into the mass of curls and find out if they really felt as silky as they looked.

My attraction to her had been immediate, and it wasn't all just physical. There was something about her that was...different.

"Not the brunette," Mason answered in a strange baritone I'd never heard before. "The blonde."

Damned if I didn't heave a sigh of relief when my brother acknowledged that he liked the pretty blonde next to my temptress. "Should we introduce ourselves?" I asked.

My brother tore his eyes away from the female he was apparently attracted to and looked back at me. "I'm not into stalking women, Carter."

"It's not stalking," I scoffed. "It's called being social."

"Then I guess I'm not *social*," he rumbled as he downed half his drink. "I'm heading for the office."

I glanced at my expensive watch. "Now? It's after ten."

"I have clothes there, and I have work I need to do," Mason answered.

"No, you really don't," I disagreed. "Mason, we hired a CEO so we could all slow down."

After our younger brother, Jett, had gotten engaged, we'd all agreed to stop working twenty-four-seven most of the time. The idea was to get together with our two sisters in Colorado more often, and have a life.

Lawson had made me and my two brothers billionaires many times over, but not without sacrificing everything else in our lives, including family. My sisters were married and settled. Jett was engaged, and he wanted to free himself up to spend more time with his fiancée, Ruby. My younger brother also wanted his family back. Even though Mason, Jett, and I ran the same business, we very rarely spent any time doing family things. It was all business, and we ran different areas of Lawson, which meant we rarely saw each other, even though we worked at the same address.

Jett was the visionary and the cyber-security expert.

I was the marketing behind the company.

And Mason was pretty much everything else that had to do with growing our tech giant. He'd made us global, and he was still working to conquer the countries where Lawson wasn't a household name.

"I'm going to Jett and Ruby's engagement party," Mason said, like he was accomplishing a major feat. "Although I still don't get why they're having it now. They've been engaged for months."

"Ruby is still pretty young," I drawled. "But Jett wants to celebrate. And he doesn't want to marry her too quickly because of her past. He wants to give her time to find herself."

If you asked me, my younger brother was having one hell of a time not tying the knot. But I had to respect the fact that he didn't want to push his twenty-three-year-old fiancée because she came from a life of abuse and homelessness.

Not that Ruby didn't know her own mind. I'd discovered *that* when I'd tried to break the two of them up. I'd thought she was just using my wealthy but scarred little brother.

But for once in my life, I was actually wrong.

I'd gotten a wake-up call from Ruby that I'd never forgotten, and probably never would. Despite the fact that Jett limped when he overexerted, and he lived with the scars of a near-fatal helicopter crash a few years ago, Ruby loved him with all her heart.

And I believed that now without a doubt.

What had seemed illogical and unlikely actually made sense now.

My younger brother and his even younger fiancée belonged together.

"She loves him," Mason grunted, sounding satisfied. "Ruby is good for Jett."

"Agreed."

"But I still don't get why they need a party," he said, and then tossed back the rest of his drink. "It's a waste of time. The engagement is already done."

I smirked. I was pretty sure Mason *never* saw a reason to celebrate. "You don't have to understand," I informed him. "But you need to show up. Danica and Harper are coming into town with their husbands for it, and you won't be forgiven for missing the event."

"I'm going," he said, looking slightly pained. "I won't miss the chance to see the whole family together."

I believed him. Once Mason gave his word, he never broke it. "Go home," I advised him, noticing that he looked weary. "Leave some of the business to our CEO and the executives. We don't need to keep working every moment of the day that we aren't sleeping anymore."

Mason shrugged his broad shoulders. "What else is there to do?"

I polished off my drink and sat it on the bar, and then folded my arms in front of me.

My elder brother had always been the serious one. But he hadn't always been *this* detached. No doubt that spending every waking hour at Lawson had made him this way. But it was beyond time for him to slow things down.

He looked completely wiped out, and he needed to find some kind of pleasure in his life other than stressing over a company that could run just fine without all of us if it needed to.

Hell, I wasn't asking him to give up being part of Lawson. All three of us had nurtured our company into a worldwide juggernaut.

Back then, it had been necessary.

Now, it wasn't.

Truthfully, I was starting to feel the need for our family to pull together again just like my brother, Jett. Not that I admitted that to him, but I could see how far we'd all drifted apart.

We'd all grown up in Rocky Springs, Colorado. But when our parents had died in a car accident, we'd all handled their deaths differently.

We'd all done our grieving in very different ways.

Now, it was fucking time for us to be a family again.

I knew damn well that we all missed each other, even though we'd never drawn together to get through the tragedy of our parents' deaths. Maybe we'd needed our space to lick our wounds separately. But dammit, we were family, and it was time for us to act like one.

Yeah, we were there for each other when we needed to be. But what the hell had happened to us all being there for the good stuff, too?

"There's plenty of other things in life except work," I advised. Not that I really knew that many of those particular activities myself, but I wanted to make a life outside of work, too.

"What exactly?" Mason asked, one brow up in question.

"Love?" I asked. "Maybe what our sisters and Jett have now? Maybe caring about something except our damn company."

Maybe I *shouldn't* talk. I'd been a workaholic right along with my two brothers. But something had happened to me a few years ago, and it wasn't good. When Jett had gotten into his accident, and we were waiting to see if he was going to live or die, I'd realized how little I'd paid attention to the world around me.

Unfortunately, I'd turned into an unhappy dick, looking for my pleasure in alcohol, women, and shit that got me into nothing but trouble.

I'd hated myself for not protecting my little brother better, so I'd gone into overdrive protective mode to keep him safe once we realized he was going to live, but that he'd be scarred and damaged for life. I'd tried to draw a wedge between him and Ruby because I didn't want to see Jett get used by a woman who could drain him dry and leave him even more broken.

Problem was, Ruby had changed Jett's life in the best of ways. I'd just been too stupid to tell that the woman loved him unconditionally.

I was doing everything I could now to make up for the mistake I'd made.

Maybe I'd ended up falling a little bit in love with Ruby myself. Not in an intimate way, but in the same way I cared about and admired my own sisters.

"Love is for men like Jett," Mason said unhappily. "Fuck knows he deserves it."

"Does that mean we're too jaded for that?" I asked.

I *was* a lost cause. I was too far gone and way too cynical for something like Jett had with Ruby. But maybe I could learn not to be quite as big of a dick as I used to be.

"I am," Mason said gruffly. "The verdict is still out about you."

I shrugged. "I'm not the type to fall in love. It will never happen. But I'd like to see our family happy and together again."

"I suppose I would, too," Mason answered with a hint of regret in his voice.

"We'll get there eventually," I told him. "All of us just got too involved in our lives and forgot we were part of a family."

Mason folded his bulky arms across his chest. "Can we fix it? Hell, I'm thirty-four years old, and you're just two years behind me. We've missed a lot."

I grinned at him. "We're not exactly old. And yes, I think if we *want* to put our family back together again, we can."

Was there even an age when it was too late to mend a family? I didn't think so. Maybe a year ago, I would have had as many doubts as Mason. But after a few come-to-Jesus moments with Jett over the last few months and right after his accident, I was pretty sure we *could* all be a family again.

We just needed to figure out how to do it without our parents.

But I think we'd all had enough time to realize that our parents were never coming back, and all we had was each other.

We'd all been close as kids.

But we'd...lost each other.

Mason slapped me on the shoulder. "I'm out of here."

"Go home," I insisted.

"We'll see," he answered vaguely.

I was pretty sure that meant he was going to the office.

"I think I'll stay for a while," I answered, my eyes drawn to the vivacious brunette again.

There hadn't been a single moment tonight that I wasn't aware of her. Not from the instant I'd seen her.

"You're going to keep stalking?" he asked.

"Observing," I corrected.

"Keep your eyes off the sexy blonde," he insisted. "She looks way too sweet for you."

"She's all yours," I informed him.

"I wish. She's definitely too angelic for me," he grumbled as he turned and walked away.

I smirked as I watched him make his way to the entrance and then disappear, pretty sure that his interest in the blonde woman would fade as soon as he got to his office and started working.

I had to wonder again if my brother ever got any action. If he didn't, it was no wonder that he was so damn irritable.

Turning away from Mason's departing figure, I went to focus on my mission, which was to meet the only woman who had caught my eye in a very long time.

I wanted her in my bed.

And I was used to getting exactly what I desired.

"Fuck!" I cursed, realizing that while my attention had been on my older brother, the woman I'd wanted to meet all damn night was gone.

Chapter 3

Brynn

Later that evening, I sighed as I looked out the enormous picture window of my new condo.

I'd just moved in, and I was completely content with my choice. I was only a few blocks from the boutique, and looking out the huge window in my living room, which was so high above the city, was incredibly peaceful.

Silent chaos.

The hustle and bustle below was soundless on the top floors of the condo high-rise. There was something magical about seeing all the lights and commotion of the city, but not hearing it.

The condo had a beautiful western view of the Puget Sound, and the city was spread out for miles beneath me.

Here in my home, I felt safe. I was just an observer when I was this far above the madness of the city.

Laura's condo wasn't far away, and I'd enjoyed staying with her until I found my own place, but I was happy to finally find and purchase my own condo that I could call home.

The walls were now filled with pictures, years of experiences I'd had in different countries all over the world.

I smiled as I looked over the images of me and my mother in my younger days of modeling.

One of the pleasures I had from my long, successful modeling career was knowing that my only close family member was safe, and in a beautiful house in my home state of Michigan.

My heart hurt just a little because I hadn't seen my mother in over a year, but I'd get back to Michigan soon to visit.

I'd tried to convince her to relocate to Seattle with me, but Mom had spent her entire life in Michigan, and she didn't want to leave.

I understood why she hadn't wanted to move, but we'd spent so much of my adult life apart that I guess I'd been hoping we'd finally be in the same city.

But Michigan was familiar to her, and she was happy there. Honestly, I was pretty sure she'd hate living in a big city after a lifetime of being in a more rural area.

Unfortunately, even knowing she was content, I still felt the pain of missing her sometimes. But at least I had those memories of traveling with her early in my career.

I'd been discovered for modeling at the age of sixteen, and she'd sacrificed everything to make sure I could get to my jobs while I'd been underage, no matter where those assignments were located.

Those later teenage years had probably been some of the happiest times of my life.

We'd gone from location to location, and seen things we never thought we'd be able to see when I went to shoots.

Unfortunately, soon after I turned eighteen, she'd been diagnosed with breast cancer, and she couldn't travel with me anymore.

Mom had gotten the best of care, and she'd had my aunt, her sister, to help her. But as her daughter, I'd wanted to be there, too. But my mother had done nothing but encourage me when my career took off. Yes, she'd let me pay to take care of her because she didn't have any other options. However, she'd insisted that my life not stop because she had cancer, and a model's life didn't allow me to spend a lot of my time in a small town in Michigan.

After a very long, six-year battle, Mom had finally won her battle with cancer, and she was still clean from the soul-eating disease that had ravaged her life.

So when I'd finally decided to slow down and put down some roots, I'd wanted nothing more than for her to join me here in Seattle because I still had a career to chase. The money still needed to come in so I could take care of my mom. But being the stubborn woman she was, my mother had insisted she was fine where she was, and that she wanted me to go to Seattle to keep reaching for something more with my career. She was happy with having her sister live with her. My Aunt Marlene had lost my uncle to a heart attack five years ago, and not only did the two of them live together, but they were thicker than thieves.

I grabbed my phone and plopped down on the sofa, and then dialed my mom's number. Seattle was three hours behind Michigan time, but my parent tended to be a night owl.

"Hi honey." My mother picked up the phone after the first ring. "Everything okay?"

"I'm good," I acknowledged. "I was just missing you."

"I miss you, too, Brynn," she said softly. "But I'm so proud of you."

I smiled. Mom had always been my biggest fan. "You sound wide awake," I observed.

"I just got home. I went out for coffee and pie with Mick."

"You're still seeing him?" I asked, concerned.

Mick had been in my mother's life for over a year. She said they were friends, but I had to wonder if there was something more there for both of them.

Even though I wanted her to be happy, I was skeptical of any male who was hanging out with my mom. Not that she wasn't still beautiful, and she was a bright light that a man would notice.

But her past history made any man suspect in my eyes.

"Mom, are you sure this isn't something more than a friendship?" I didn't want anybody to hurt her.

I'd learned to hide my own insecurities deep inside me, but my mother had never changed. She was still an open book, and wore her emotions on her sleeve all the time.

"And if it is?" she asked cautiously.

I sighed. "Then I'd be worried."

"Brynn, Mick has his own money. That's not what he's looking for."

"It's not that," I confessed. "I just don't want to see you disappointed."

"Oh, honey," she crooned. "Please don't let what happened—"

"I'm not," I said hurriedly, well aware that I was lying.

"Are you seeing anyone?" she said skeptically.

"No, Mom. I'm too involved in my career. I travel. I'm busy."

"You're not traveling as much, and you're settling down," she reminded me. "I'd really love to see a grandchild before I get too old to play with him or her."

"Don't hold your breath," I said lightly. "There's nobody."

Really, there never had been. I dated, but when things got too serious, I sprinted from the relationship.

I liked sex as much as any woman did, but the entanglements of having a relationship were way too stifling.

"Not all men suck, Brynn," she nudged me.

In my experience, they did. But I answered, "I know, Mom."

I hadn't let a man get close to me for well over a decade, and I didn't see it happening anytime soon. Honestly, I didn't think I'd *ever* see it.

I dated casually.

I had sex if I wanted it.

And then I walked away.

It was safer that way.

We chatted for a while about friends and family in Michigan, the weather, the boutique, and a myriad of other things before we got ready to hang up.

"Don't let your past decide your future," my mother warned ominously.

"I won't," I agreed readily, even though I knew I was still fighting my demons.

Mom was ready to move on.

I wasn't sure if I ever would be.

"I love you," I told her.

"I love you, too, honey. Try to work on those grandchildren. You're my only child."

Oh Lord, the guilt. "Sure, Mom."

We disconnected and I tossed my cell onto the table in front of the couch.

I picked up a huge throw pillow and hugged it against my body.

My mother was always the only person I could count on, except for Laura.

I didn't need a man to complete my life.

I was okay with who I was, but lately, I was feeling a lot lonelier than I ever had. Maybe it was the change in location. I didn't have as many friends and acquaintances here in Seattle. I'd left them all behind when I'd moved out of New York City.

I missed the parties.

I missed constantly being so busy that I didn't have to think.

New York was full of people I knew who would go visit an exhibition, a show, go for drinks, or any other activity that would consume my thoughts for a time.

Seattle actually felt more like home, and for me, I was discovering the sense of being settled was actually…dangerous.

I thought too much about my life now.

I thought too much about my future.

Moving here had been the first real opportunity I'd had to really consider the fact that my modeling career would end someday. And I really needed to be thinking about my future.

Sure, I was still the recognizable face for Easily Beautiful, one of the biggest luxury cosmetic companies in existence. And I had a lucrative contract that wouldn't be over for another year.

Not that I really had to worry about money. My lengthy stint as a successful model had made me wealthy, but even better, it had kept me so busy traveling and making appearances that I hadn't had time to think.

Now, I did.

And it pretty much sucked.

I closed my eyes and took a couple of deep breaths in and out.

Living in a state of mindfulness had helped me get through all those years of career craziness.

Don't worry about the past.

Don't stress over the future.

All I really have is right now.

I tried to be *present*, living in the current moment, in touch with how I was taking up space and existing in the world around me.

I kept breathing, trying to connect my mind and body.

It had always worked for me.

Unfortunately, I didn't get the peace I craved. My brain was too determined to think, and I couldn't seem to make those negative thoughts vanish.

Chapter 4

Brynn

I woke up early the next morning, and immediately got ready to hit the state-of-the-art gym I had in my condo complex.

I'd never been the type of woman who lived in a melancholy state, and I wasn't about to start now.

Doing my exercise would help me get back to normal. At least I hoped it would.

I stuffed my swimsuit in my duffel bag. I didn't pay enormous association dues for nothing. My condo came with every imaginable amenity, and I planned to take advantage of every single one of them.

I did a short meditation in my condo, and then some relaxing yoga, forcing my mind away from anything except the present, and then snatched my bag and headed for the door.

After locking up, I headed for the elevator—no way was I traipsing up and down twenty-three stories of stairs every single day. Maybe I wanted to be fit, but I wasn't a masochist.

I regretted my decision the moment the doors opened with a *swoosh* and I looked at exactly what—or should I say who?—was inside the lift.

Every damn female hormone in my body stood up and took notice the second Carter Lawson grinned at me.

My skintight, stretchy workout pants and the tank I was wearing suddenly made me feel like I was naked. Correction—the way he *looked at me* stripped me bare.

Just like it had at the cocktail party.

I hated the fact that Carter was deliciously handsome, and deca-dently dangerous.

My body riveted in place, and he had to motion to me to get into the elevator.

I finally stepped in, annoyed with myself. I didn't even *know* the man. Maybe he *was* drop-dead gorgeous, but there was no reason for me to let him affect me. *None whatsoever.*

It wasn't like I didn't see beautiful men in my profession.

I saw the hottest of the hot male models all the time, and even did shoots or commercials with them.

But none of them had ever made my nipples get this painfully hard with a casual glance. And I'd certainly never had the urge to climb any of them like a tree and beg them to take away the sharp pain of desire that seized me with a single look from Carter.

His eyes are so damn blue.

The man had already won the genetic lotto. Why did he have to have such gorgeous eyes?

I tore my gaze away from his as I leaned against the opposite wall, ignoring him.

The difficulty was, once the door closed, I could *smell* him. I could *sense* him. And I sure as hell couldn't forget what he looked like in that custom dark-blue suit that matched his eyes.

"Headed for the gym?" he asked in a casual baritone that seemed to vibrate through my entire body.

His voice was like fine whiskey and sin, and so much sexier than I ever could have conjured up in my mind.

"Yes," I replied. My retort had a lot more angst than I would have liked. "And the pool."

"Nice facilities," he mentioned. "Lived here long? I've never seen you."

Why did his comment about the workout facilities feel like something way different?

I'm starting to imagine things.

I still didn't look at him because he made me uneasy, but I could feel his gaze on me.

I shrugged. "I bought a place here. Just moved in last week."

I really wanted him to stop talking. His voice was like a mating call to me, and I was definitely in heat.

"I'm in the penthouse," he drawled.

Yeah. Of course he was. Probably nobody except a billionaire could afford the luxurious dwelling that took up the entire top floor.

I finally looked at him, but regretted it almost immediately. A disconcerting *pop!* ran down my spine, zinging in every single vertebra until all that energy finally pooled directly between my thighs. "Don't you have your own elevator?" I snapped, pissed off because I sounded so irritable.

His smile got broader, like he knew how his presence in the enclosed car was getting to me, and then shrugged. "They're doing maintenance on it."

And, just like me, there was no way *he* was going to take the stairs. Not that I could blame him. He looked like he was dressed for work, not a single hair out of place.

I searched for an imperfection that would make him seen more human, but I couldn't find a single one. Somehow, I had a feeling everything Carter Lawson did was cool and calculated.

"How sad for you," I countered in a slightly sarcastic tone.

Jesus! I needed to get out of the elevator. The short ride had turned me into a raving bitch.

All that training to always be nice in public had apparently disappeared.

The way I felt when I was in close proximity to Carter made me so edgy that I could do nothing more than count every millisecond until I could make my escape.

I was just about ready to breathe a sigh of relief when the elevator stuttered to a stop just before it reached the lobby.

It took me a moment to realize that his hand had slammed against the *Emergency Stop* button.

His expression was less amiable, and a lot fiercer than it had been when he'd waved me in.

My stomach lurched with the elevator as I gawked at him. "What are you doing?"

"I want to have dinner with you," he stated, as though it were an order. "We saw each other yesterday at the benefit. We connected. I know you know what I'm talking about. It has to be fate that put us in this elevator. I was going to try to find you anyway, but now you're here, and we live in the same damn building."

"Why do we have to pursue it?" I said breathlessly as he moved closer. "And I don't believe in fate. We make our own destiny."

"I usually don't either," he grumbled. "I'm the last person who'd ever leave anything to chance."

"I'm busy," I told him in a rush.

"Tonight?" he asked with a frown.

"Every night," I answered as he crowded me.

Carter pinned me in with a hand resting on each side of my head, his body so close that I nearly groaned.

"Bullshit," he growled. "You're as damn intrigued as I am. We're feeling the same chemistry. I don't fucking understand it, but I want to. And I think you do, too."

"Maybe I just don't like you. I don't like pushy men," I snapped. "Please get the elevator moving. I'm sure the malfunction has already gone to the front desk. They'll call the fire department."

"I don't give a shit," he answered. "Say you'll have dinner with me and I'll push the button in a heartbeat."

I had to tilt my head slightly to look at him, which was saying something for a model who often towered over a lot of guys. "Not interested," I said firmly, but with some desperation that I couldn't keep out of my tone.

He smelled like sandalwood and alpha male, a scent that was entirely intoxicating, and I hated myself for wanting to drown in the pleasure my senses were experiencing.

But the thing that really got to me was his eyes. They'd turned a molten blue, and there was a barely discernible glint of longing there, a feeling that somehow sparked something inside me, too.

"Dinner," he insisted.

"No," I shot back.

"Then I definitely need this," he said, his warm breath drifting over my lips before he swooped down and stole my mouth.

As natural as breathing, I parted my lips and let him consume me. I felt cocooned in a world that only contained Carter, and I felt so damn alive as he conquered and took control of my every emotion.

I'd been kissed. Many times. But never in the tantalizing way that Carter was devouring me right now.

He teased.

He nipped at my lips when he was done, promising a world of pleasure like I'd never visited before.

Nothing touched except our lips, but he didn't *need* to make connection anywhere else. His warm, delicious mouth had completely made me his prisoner.

"Stop," I finally squealed after I'd turned my head in a panic, pushing desperately against his massive bulk.

He pushed with his palms, putting distance between us, letting me free, but I still felt caught up in his delicious aura.

I scrambled to push the button that would get us moving again.

I have to get out of here. I have to escape.

I dashed out of the elevator the second the doors opened, ignoring the building staff who seemed confused as to why the lift had come to a halt.

"Wait!" I heard Carter's voice call behind me. "I'm sorry," he said as he caught my upper arm, keeping me from continuing to move down the hallway to the gym.

I spun to face him, angry now that I wasn't trapped in a small space with him. "If you touch me again, I'll put you on the floor with pepper spray," I warned.

He looked surprised. "You have mace?"

Of course I had mace. I'd lived in New York City. I had a stun gun too, even though they'd been illegal there. "Yes," I answered slowly, not taking my eyes off him.

"Did I scare you?"

"No," I denied. I was such a liar.

Carter didn't frighten me in regard to my personal safety, but he terrified me in a far different way. Instinctively, I was pretty sure he wouldn't physically harm me, but I wasn't willing to take a risk with my emotional health. He did something to me that scared the hell out of me.

I didn't lose control.

I didn't just give in to a man. *Not ever.*

And I sure as hell never kissed a stranger in a damn elevator.

I kept my distance from him, pulling my arm from his grasp, but refusing to back down. Thank God there was almost nobody in the hallway to the gym. Most people were headed to work by now.

Carter frowned. "Look, I don't know what just happened. I really did just want to have dinner, but I'm weirdly attracted to you in a way I don't even understand. My name is Carter—"

"Lawson," I finished. "Co-owner of Lawson Technologies, along with your two brothers, Jett and Mason. I know who you are. And I'm still not interested."

"Then how do you know me if you've never been *interested?*"

"Oh, it isn't that I've never paid attention," I informed him. "It just so happens that I was a very early investor in Lawson Technologies. I threw a lot of money into your corporation as soon as it went public. I do my homework."

His lips turned up slightly. "You have me at a disadvantage then."

"I bet that doesn't happen often," I mumbled.

"Hardly ever," he confirmed.

It took me seeing a gym-goer giving us a puzzled look before I realized that we were in a public place, exchanging barbs.

Granted, he never should have kissed me, but I could have easily gotten free. The minute he realized I wasn't willing anymore, he'd backed off.

I wasn't the type of woman who scurried off in fear. Carter Lawson had just caught me unaware. "Brynn Davis," I said, reluctantly putting my hand out.

He took it immediately. "Truce?" he asked.

I raised a brow at him. "For now. Just don't kiss me again."

"No promises on that," he said as he slowly released my hand. "But you'll be a completely willing participant next time. I can guarantee it. I'll even ask your permission first."

God, the man could be charming. I was pretty sure he could convince a Seattleite that the city needed more rain and less sunshine if he really wanted to. "Very unlikely that I'd ever give you permission," I retorted.

He stared at me for a moment before he asked, "Brynn Davis? The supermodel?"

I nodded.

"Didn't you do some ads for Lawson? Maybe that's why you look so familiar."

I had. I was impressed that he remembered my name if not my face. "I did. But it was years ago."

I'd been thrilled to be working on a Lawson ad campaign since I was heavily invested in the company. But I'd been glad when they'd gone in another direction and focused more on the technology instead of trying to make the company sexy.

"Not that many years ago," he mused. "And all the more reason why you should have dinner with me. We have past connections."

There was that mysterious smile again, the one that made me squirm.

I replied, "An investor and previous model for your brand isn't what I'd call a *past connection*."

"It could be," he said hopefully.

Yep. Completely charming.

"Still not interested. I don't have time to date. I'm busy. I'm starting my own fashion line with a friend, and I still have modeling commitments."

"Who said it was a date?" he said in a voice that almost sounded innocent. "It's just dinner."

I stepped forward and straightened his tie for some reason. It had probably gone askew when he'd kissed me in the elevator, and it somehow seemed *off* since the man was always meticulously put together. I patted his lapel when he looked perfect again. "Have a good day at work, Mr. Lawson. Keep making money for your investors. I'm hitting the gym."

"I won't stop trying," he warned as I turned to continue on my way.

I finally smiled because my back was to him. "And I'll keep saying no," I muttered as I walked away.

Carter obviously hadn't succeeded in life without being tenacious. Fortunately, I could be just as stubborn.

Chapter 5

Carter

"I kissed a woman in the elevator today," I shared with my brothers Mason and Jett later that day in my office. "I didn't really know her, but she got to me."

I wasn't one to confess my sins to my brothers, mostly because they'd eventually use them against me to piss me off.

But my head was still reeling about what had happened that morning, and I was still perplexed about exactly why I'd felt compelled to kiss Brynn Davis. It wasn't like I was usually a pervert who ran around kissing any woman I wanted.

I was a whole lot more sophisticated and subtle.

At the risk of sounding conceited, I can honestly say that I have no problem finding a woman when I wanted one. What in the hell had I been thinking to hit on the one single female in Seattle who *wasn't* interested?

But see...maybe that *was* the problem. She was a challenge, and I hadn't had one of those in a very long time.

However, I hadn't known she wasn't going to be into me when I'd first seen her, and that was confusing since I'd known that I wanted her in my bed since we'd locked eyes at the charity benefit.

I don't chase after women. I didn't need to. And I sure as hell had never kissed a female unless I knew she was willing. I felt like my body and mind had suddenly been temporarily taken over, and some Carter I didn't know had kissed Brynn Davis.

Mason cocked a brow. "How do you know she gets to you if you don't know her?"

"Remember the two women we saw at the benefit?" I asked.

"Yeah," he answered, sounding confused.

I let out a sigh and leaned back in my desk chair. "It was her. I found out that she lives in the same building I do."

"The dark-haired woman?" he questioned.

I nodded unhappily. "Turns out she's even more beautiful and irresistible closer up."

Brynn Davis had grabbed me by the balls the second her beautiful dark eyes had connected with mine, and I'd completely lost it.

"What happened after that?" Jett asked.

I shrugged. "She blew me off."

I heard Mason chuckle—which was odd for him—right before he answered, "So she turned you down?"

"I asked her out for dinner, and she refused."

"Whoa. What did it feel like to actually suffer rejection?" Jett joked. "I think it's probably been a while for you."

I shot my little brother a dirty look. "Probably high school, and it sucked."

Women generally were falling all over themselves to meet me. And I'm not saying that because I'm arrogant. It was just...the truth.

When a guy is single and ultra-wealthy, females generally want to take a shot at getting that man to commit.

Problem was, commitment was something I avoided like a poisonous snake. *No* woman was ever going to get me into that kind of relationship. I was pretty sure I'd feel suffocated.

"What's she like?" Mason asked curiously. "And what's the deal with her blonde friend?"

"She's a supermodel. Brynn Davis. She did a shoot for one of our ads several years ago. But we could never get her agent to pin her down with a contract, and we eventually headed in another direction. She's beautiful, and she's smart."

She also hates me! I purposely didn't tell my brothers *that* part.

"And the blonde?" Mason repeated, sounding irritated.

Ah, interesting. Mason *hadn't* forgotten the pretty blonde.

"I assume she's a model, too. I'm not sure, actually. Brynn and I didn't exactly trade life stories," I grumbled. "She was pissed."

"Who did you not trade life stories with? And who was mad at you?" my brother Jett's fiancée asked as she breezed through the open door of my office, apparently in search of her fiancé.

I cringed just a little as I looked at Ruby's cheerful expression. I still felt guilty about the shitty things I'd done to her in the past.

Now, Ruby was my biggest supporter, and I had to admit that I pretty much adored her like she was one of my sisters. I was certain that nobody could dislike Ruby for an extended period of time. She was young, but intelligent. And probably the sweetest woman on the planet, regardless of the hard life she'd lived before she'd met Jett.

And bonus…she'd forgiven me for being such an asshole.

"Some woman dissed him today after he kissed her in the elevator of his condo complex," my younger brother explained.

"She did?" Ruby said as she glanced at me with concern. "Did you really do that?"

I nodded.

She smacked Jett on the arm as she sat in the chair next to him. "Stop teasing Carter. Being rejected isn't funny." She moved her gaze to me. "Are you okay?"

I was starting to feel uncomfortable. Spilling my guts about *any-thing* wasn't normal for me. "I'll live," I told Ruby with a grin. "Every guy gets rejected occasionally."

Damned if my spirits didn't lift a little as she gave me a sunny smile.

Ruby had a way of making me talk. I think it was because she cared so much, and asked a lot of questions. So I wasn't surprised when she asked, "Why did you kiss her? And how did you meet?"

Surprisingly, Mason was the one who explained that Brynn and I had seen each other at a charity benefit, and that we really hadn't met until *after* I'd kissed her.

"Maybe you shouldn't have trapped her in an elevator," Ruby finally said. "You could have scared her off. And honestly, Carter, you had no business touching her like that."

She was right, and I still felt pretty damn guilty about just taking what I wanted without thinking about how my actions might have caused unnecessary hostility between myself and Brynn.

The only thing I could do was plead temporary insanity, which kind of sounded like the truth anyway.

"I don't even know why I did that," I confessed. "One minute I was fantasizing about getting her into my bed, and the next I was kissing her. I have no idea what the hell happened."

I wasn't the type of man to accost women in an elevator.

Women came to *me*.

I didn't chase *them*.

"Sometimes you just know when you find the right person," Ruby said whimsically as she shot her fiancé an adoring look.

Since I didn't want to burst Ruby's bubble, and see disappointment on her face, I kept silent.

I wanted to *fuck* the beautiful model; I didn't exactly want a *romance*.

Somehow, I needed to get Brynn Davis out of my system. I'd been thinking about her all damn day, and it was distracting me from my work. And *that* was something that *never* happened.

I usually just got laid, and my fuck buddy was promptly forgotten. They never took my attention away from my company.

Granted, I'd temporarily lost my mind this morning, but there was something different about Brynn. I just couldn't put a finger on exactly what that *something* was.

Mason snorted before he said, "I don't think he's looking for love, Ruby."

She glared at my older brother. "You don't know that, Mason. And love isn't something anybody plans. It just…happens. In all honesty, I think you and Carter could both use a woman who isn't going to let you push them around."

I snickered as I glanced at Mason and noticed that he was actually squirming.

"I just had to kiss her. It wasn't a planned-out idea. And I regretted the impulse when she sprinted out of the elevator like I was some kind of damn monster."

"You could apologize for being a jerk," Ruby suggested.

"I never apologize for being an asshole," I informed her.

Okay. Yeah. I *had* said a quick, impulsive *I'm sorry* to Brynn, but I hadn't sincerely apologized the way I could have. Being contrite wasn't really in my nature.

Ruby folded her arms in front of her. "You could start. You obviously like her, and kissing her while she was pretty much defenseless was crossing the line."

I wasn't about to inform my sister-in-law-to-be that I'd actually *stopped* said elevator before I'd kissed Brynn. She didn't really need to know that. "What I really need is to forget about it."

Unlike Jett, I wasn't cut out to be monogamous. It wasn't that I felt like I needed a different woman all the time. It was a case of me not having the time or the desire to keep one female happy.

Building Lawson Technologies had been my life for most of my adult years, and I didn't know how to do anything else. So, in some ways, I could relate to Mason. Any other priorities were always a distant second place for me, and I had no idea how to change that, either. Until now, I'd never had the desire to do anything except play the business game.

Ruby shot me a disappointed look as she stood up. "Jett and I have dinner plans, so we have to go. We're trying out a new restaurant. But I think you should think about apologizing, Carter. I've never seen you have this kind of interest in a woman before, and I don't think you should blow it with her."

News flash: I'd already blown it. Ruby hadn't seen the obstinate look on Brynn's face when we'd parted this morning.

But Ruby was probably never going to understand that I didn't covet a relationship like she had with Jett.

I liked my freedom.

"I'll think about it," I agreed vaguely.

I watched as Ruby, Jett, and Mason departed, and then leaned back in my comfortable office chair with a sigh.

Apologize? Oh, hell no. I was Carter Lawson, a man known for playing the game better than everyone else. I was *never* sorry, and I sure as fuck wasn't asking anybody to forgive me.

But God, Brynn Davis was tempting enough to make me flirt with the idea.

Would it help? Probably not.

She'd been pretty adamant about not wanting to go to dinner.

For fuck's sake, Lawson, forget about it!

Problem was, the memory of her stubborn expression, her fearless stance when she'd finally spoken to me, and her beautiful, dark, exotic eyes had haunted me all day.

She's a supermodel. She's attractive. That's it.

Strangely, I didn't like the fact that men were probably ogling her all the time. Brynn Davis was probably the star player in a large number of men's fantasies, and *that* irritated the hell out of me, too.

Leaning forward again, I opened the merger file on my desk.

"Fuck!" I said to myself in a disgusted voice. "What in the hell am I doing?"

I had a ton of work to get done before I could leave the office.

I'd spilled about what I'd done this morning to my brothers and Ruby, hoping for some kind of damn advice.

And I was actually *thinking* about sincerely apologizing to Brynn.

I told her I was sorry. That should be enough, right? She knew.

I specifically remembered that I'd blurted out those two little words as soon as I'd caught up with her after she'd bolted from the elevator.

It was unusual for me to say I was sorry at all. In fact, I couldn't remember a time that I had since I'd become a grown adult.

As I focused on the paperwork I had to review, I tried to push her out of my brain completely.

There were other women.

Plenty of them.

I didn't need to obsess over a single female who just wasn't interested in me. That would make me pretty damn pathetic.

I finished my work several hours later, and realized that I hadn't been completely successful at writing Brynn Davis off.

Maybe because I wanted her way too much.

Chapter 6

Brynn

I decided to take a jog the next morning instead of sticking with my usual exercise routine.

I might not be a fast runner, but I enjoyed being outside in the early morning.

After I'd walked to Myrtle Edwards Park, I'd started a slow but steady pace along the waterfront. There were already people out biking, walking, and jogging, but it wasn't as crowded as it probably would be later in the day.

I pulled down the brim of my baseball cap. I'd put my hair in a ponytail and stuck it through the back of the hat. The hat had a dual purpose: it kept the sun off my face, and it hid my identity.

If I didn't want to be recognized, I usually wasn't. People saw what they wanted to see. If I wasn't in full makeup, nobody really paid attention. I looked just like any other person jogging on a nice day in Seattle.

It was funny to live in the city, yet have so many places to take a peaceful run.

Really, I *needed* to chill out. I hadn't relaxed since my run-in with Carter yesterday.

Why in the hell had he just...kissed me like that?

In all the articles I'd read about him in the past, I'd never seen a word about him being pushy with women, or assaulting one when she wasn't expecting it.

I'd wanted it as much as he did.

Not that I was making excuses for him, but I had a feeling that my eyes had been begging him to touch me. And he had.

If it had been any other guy, I would have kneed him in the balls for touching me, but for some reason, with Carter, it had come so naturally that I hadn't questioned it until it was over.

I tried to get my breathing under control as I increased my pace. But the sound of my own footsteps rhythmically hitting the pavement didn't drown out my thoughts about the man who had rocked my world with a simple embrace.

Don't, Brynn. Don't romanticize it. You know better. You're a practical woman.

I felt my phone vibrate on my ass. I pulled it from the small back pocket of my exercise pants, happy for any kind of distraction.

I smiled as I saw that the text was from Laura. She'd found a new Korean restaurant, and wanted to meet up for lunch to talk about one of her designs.

Last night, I'd found myself straying from our typical clothing, and started to plan out a handbag design that actually made sense. For me, designer bags weren't the least bit functional, so I'd drawn up a purse that I thought would be amazing for women who wanted a bag that worked. I'd gotten caught up in designing a purse that was actually perfect for a woman who traveled.

Stylish and functional *could* go together. Women didn't need to sacrifice one for the other.

But I had a whole closet full of mistakes because I'd been looking for just that.

I wanted to talk to Laura about what I'd designed.

It was during the moment I tried to text back to her that I realized that jogging and texting might be as dangerous as driving and texting.

My message never got sent.

Instead, I found myself colliding with a very solid wall, and I let out a yelp of pain as I bounced backward and landed flat on my ass several paces back from where I'd had my mishap.

My hands went behind me to brace my fall, but my head still slammed into the pavement.

"Dammit," I hissed as I tried to sit up while I was still dizzy from the impact.

I rolled into the dirt as I saw the approach of a bicycle that looked determined to run over me.

"Brynn, are you hurt?" I heard a familiar baritone ask in a gruff tone.

I closed my eyes to rub the back of my head, but I opened them again, and saw Carter Lawson crouching down beside me.

I blinked several times, but the image didn't go away.

He was dressed in a pair of jogging pants and a t-shirt. Apparently, judging by his disheveled appearance, he'd been doing the same thing I was in the park.

I moaned. "What happened?"

He gingerly touched the back of my head. "It was you versus me. I won by a pretty large margin. Why in the hell were you using your phone? I moved to avoid you, but you came right across the path so quickly that I couldn't avoid you. Are you okay?"

I looked around me, realizing that I had definitely crossed to the opposite side as I was trying to text. I was embarrassed. "I'll live," I answered as I struggled to get to my feet.

I'd finally figured out that *Carter* was the solid brick wall I'd collided with.

My ankle gave out on me as I rose, and I would have hit the ground again if Carter hadn't wrapped a powerful arm around my waist. "You're hurt. Your head is bleeding, and you're limping. Your ankle?"

I nodded. "I think I sprained it. It hurts."

"You injured your head, too. I saw you hit the ground," he said grimly. "We need to get you checked out."

"I'll be fine," I said hurriedly.

"You're not *fine*," he said, the look in his eyes stubborn.

I felt like an idiot. Not only had I managed to slam into Carter Lawson—literally—but I'd injured myself, too.

"I'll get it checked out later," I promised.

I knew I had to find a way to look like I wasn't hurting as I made my way very ungracefully down the side of the bike and walking path.

I could walk, but it hurt to do it.

"What in the hell do you think you're doing?" Carter growled as he easily caught up to me.

"I need to get home," I replied.

"You can't walk on that ankle. Don't be stubborn, Brynn. You'll just make it worse."

I stopped and faced him. "What do you propose that I do? I have to get back somehow."

He crouched in front of me. "Climb up."

"You can't carry me," I argued.

"Do it," he demanded.

"Carter, it's too far back to our building."

"We aren't going far. There's a clinic just outside the park."

I didn't have much choice. I wasn't about to bring an ambulance to the park for minor injuries, and it *was* really hard to walk.

Carefully, I climbed up on Carter's body, and he put a strong hold on my legs as he straightened up.

I might be hurting, but I couldn't help but notice how powerful his body was, his muscles flexing as he easily bore the strain of holding my entire body. And I was no lightweight. I might be fit, but I was tall.

"I'm sorry," I said unhappily as he moved at a pretty fast pace for a guy who was carrying both of our body weights. "I should have stopped to use my phone."

"I guess we all make mistakes," he said, not even sounding winded.

I knew he was talking about what had happened in the elevator the day before. "My mistake was different."

"How so?" he questioned. "You invaded my space just like I invaded yours."

"It wasn't…intimate."

"The hell it wasn't," he answered. "Your leg connected with my nuts."

I closed my eyes in mortification. "I'm sorry. Did I hurt you?"

"I'd feel better if you said you forgive me for yesterday," he suggested.

He was loading on the charm, and it was annoying that I wasn't completely immune to it.

I rolled my eyes as I clung to his muscular shoulders. "Blackmail?"

He shook his head. "Not at all."

"I forgive you," I said with a smile. "So does this make us even now?"

He'd been pretty damn nice about me slamming into him, and then had even stuck around to help.

"I'm not sure," he answered. "A guy's nuts are a pretty intimate thing. But I guess we can call it even."

I smiled broader, even though I was hurting. "Thanks for this," I said softly. "I feel terrible."

The poor man had already hoofed it to the perimeter of the park, and showed no sign of slowing down.

"We'll get you fixed up, Brynn. I promise."

He thought I was talking about my pain and not my embarrassment. "I'll be okay. It's just an ankle."

I rested my aching head against his shoulder. My entire body hurt, but I wasn't about to inform Carter of that.

"I thought you used the gym," he said.

"I like to be outside. I decided to take a run instead. What were you doing here?"

I took a deep breath as I closed my eyes, hoping that the pain in my head would go away soon. But Carter's masculine scent taunted me.

It wasn't difficult to find myself wishing that my legs were wrapped around his deliciously ripped body for a far different reason.

Like it or not, I was so attracted to Carter Lawson that even though I was in pain, I couldn't control my lustful thoughts.

"I needed to clear my head with a run," he finally answered. "Now I'm kind of glad I was here. If you hadn't crashed into me, it would have been somebody else."

He was probably right. There were enough people present that I would have eventually ran into something or someone that would have stopped me. I was just grateful that it wasn't a fast-moving bicycle. That probably would have done more damage.

Strangely, I was actually happy Carter was here, too. It would have been incredibly awkward had this happened with a complete stranger.

At the moment, he was my hero.

"I'm glad you were here, too," I said softly, realizing that I truly meant it.

Chapter 7

Brynn

"It still doesn't look good," Carter said with a frown as he knelt beside my couch and plopped another ice bag on my ankle. "It's really swollen."

I didn't mention that he'd barely given the previous one a chance to start melting before he'd gone to the freezer to make another one.

He'd been so damn nice that I was actually starting to like him just a little, and that was something I definitely couldn't afford to do.

But really, what guy carries a woman on his back to get her to a doctor? And then brings her home in a limo, picks her up again to get her up to her condo, and hangs out with her to make sure she's okay?

No man I've ever met.

"It's just a sprain, Carter. I'll live," I told him.

"The doctor said you need to stay off it for at least a couple of days, more if the swelling doesn't go down," he argued.

My injuries were minor. The cut on my head was small. Apparently head wounds just bleed a lot. And my ankle was only a bad sprain.

But I had to admit that there was something kind of sweet about a man who fussed over things that weren't that big of a deal.

"I'll rest it," I promised. "You can go ahead and go. I took enough of your time today." It was afternoon, and he still hadn't left.

"I'm not leaving," he informed me as he stood up. "Someone needs to take care of you. What if you need something? You can't walk on that ankle right now."

"You don't need to stay with me," I said, my tone sounding a little bit harsh because he'd caught me off-guard.

Carter had dashed back to his condo to shower, and he'd returned in less than ten minutes. I'd been surprised that he hadn't still been dressed for the office.

He was wearing a pair of jeans and a sea-blue t-shirt that looked amazing on him.

It was funny how much more approachable the guy looked when he was dressed casually.

Honestly, there was a small part of me that *did* want him to stay. Not because I needed assistance, but because it was nice having him around. Granted, I never would have wanted to get near him again if he hadn't shown another side of himself this morning. But now that I knew he could be a decent person, I was sort of intrigued.

"Don't you have to be in the office?" I questioned as he moved toward the door.

"Lawson is going to function just fine if I'm not there," he answered as he plopped his gorgeous jean-clad ass on my sofa. "Some things are more important than work."

The look on his face told me that he was a little stunned that he'd said those words. He appeared as if he was still trying to figure out *why* he had.

"What were you doing in the park?" I asked.

He shrugged. "I've been running there for a long time."

So he wasn't the type of man who *had* to get into a gym. But it was obvious that he did that, too. Nobody had a body like his without pumping a little iron.

"Thank you for what you did," I said, knowing it was beyond time for me to tell him that I appreciated everything he'd done for me. It had been my fault that we'd collided in the first place. I should have left my cell in my pocket where it belonged.

He reached for the glass of iced tea that he'd set on the side table as he responded. "Did you think I would just leave you lying in the dirt?"

"I don't know what kind of person you are," I mused. "All I know is that you kiss women in elevators."

"I don't," he denied. "Just you."

"Why me?" I asked in a husky tone.

"I don't know," he said vaguely. "Maybe I just find you incredibly kissable."

I rolled my eyes as I reached for the Diet Coke that Carter had gotten for me. He met plenty of women, and I had no doubt he scored pretty often. It wasn't like he needed to approach any woman in an elevator, whether he found her *kissable* or not.

"So do you like what you do?" he asked, changing the subject. "Being a model?"

I shrugged. "Most of the time," I told him. "It's made me a lot of money so I could invest, and I've traveled all over the world. I couldn't have had all the experiences I've had if it wasn't for my career."

"I hear a 'but' in there somewhere," he said.

"I can't be a model forever. I'm twenty-nine years old. I have to think about the future now."

"That's not exactly elderly," he joked.

"Models have a short shelf life," I told him.

"And what kind of future do you see?"

I shot him a curious look. "Is this a job interview or casual conversation?"

He shot out questions like he was interviewing me for a position at Lawson.

"I guess I haven't had a conversation with anybody but people in my business for a while," he admitted. "But I really want to know."

Our eyes met, and I could tell he was serious. Obviously, Carter liked to control his conversations, but his earnest expression told me that he was interested in hearing what I had to say. "I'm trying to start my own fashion line. My friend Laura and I have a small boutique downtown. We're still developing the complete collection. It's a work in progress. Eventually, we'll have to scale up, but I don't think either one of us knows how to do it. And it's going to be costly, so we're taking it slow, and learning while we go along. Both of us still have modeling commitments."

"I could help you," he offered, his tone earnest. "I've kind of got some experience at scaling up a business."

I laughed. "I'd say you definitely know what you're doing. Lawson's timing was always perfect. You and your brothers always seemed to know when it was time to take a leap forward. And thanks for offering. When we're ready, I might take you up on giving us some advice."

"If you let me take you out to dinner, I'll tell you whatever you want," he said with a sly smile.

Oh, God, he's really charming when he wants to be.

His lazy grin made me smile back at him. "We'll see," I answered cautiously. "Right now, I really need to get a shower. I'm a mess."

I hadn't even changed out of my running clothes, and I was pretty sure that I was stinky.

He set his glass back on the side table. "I'll give you a hand."

He rose, closed the distance between us, and scooped me off the couch.

"Carter, I can hobble in there," I squealed.

"No need," he replied. "Just point me in the right direction."

I guided him to the en-suite bathroom attached to the master bedroom. He lowered me to the ground slowly as he said, "Don't put too much weight on it, and don't stand up for too long. You need to get that ice pack back on and sit your beautiful ass on the couch tonight."

I was breathless just from being close to him, and I hated it. I wasn't the type of woman who got excited over a guy. I'd cared about some, and slept with others when I really wanted sex, but I didn't get twitterpated over a ripped body or being close to a male. For the most part, men had come and gone from my life fairly quickly. I'd tried a long-term relationship once, but it hadn't turned out well. After that, I kept it pretty simple.

But Carter got to me for some reason. I didn't understand the connection or the gnawing feeling in my stomach when I inhaled his masculine scent, but I couldn't deny it was there.

"Thanks," I said hurriedly, trying to distance myself from him as soon as my feet hit the ground.

"You need clothes?" he asked huskily.

"I can handle it. I'll be back out in a few minutes."

The last thing I wanted was for Carter to start rummaging through my underwear drawer. It was much too intimate and personal.

I breathed a sigh of relief when he turned and strode out of the bathroom, and through the bedroom, closing the door behind him.

Disgusted with myself, I turned on the shower and then stripped. Some of the tension in my body drained away as I stepped beneath the warm shower stream.

Maybe it had been better when I hadn't liked Carter.

Now, I *was* starting to like him. How could I not after all the things he'd done for me this morning?

Yeah, he was uptight and businesslike, but I couldn't shake the feeling that there was more to Carter Lawson than met the eye. What he'd done to help me out proved it.

I still had a feeling he was a fraud, that he hid a large part of himself inside, and only let people see what he wanted them to see.

Like recognizes *like*. There was a huge portion of myself that I never let people see, either.

Maybe that's why I could spot those characteristics in him.

After I finished my shower, I stepped out, wondering if I was imagining that Carter was something he wasn't.

It could all be in my head. I was attracted to him, therefore, I had to justify the crazy feelings I experienced when I was with him.

Honestly, I had no idea why it even mattered. Carter was being sweet to me after I'd taken a tumble. It wasn't like we were dating or planning on dating.

I moved to the bedroom and quickly dressed in a fresh pair of yoga pants and a clean white tank, doing very little to my hair except pulling it back in a clip.

When I made my way back to the living room, I limped quickly to the couch, unwilling to find myself hauled up against Carter's body again.

"What are you doing?" I called out as I caught sight of Carter in the kitchen.

"Dinner," he answered simply, his voice easily carrying from the kitchen to the living room due to the open floor plan of my condo. I could see him moving around at the counter.

I flopped back down on the sofa, and picked up the fresh ice bag that he had obviously left there for me. "You're cooking?"

He emerged from the kitchen carrying two plates and some napkins. "I don't cook, and you wouldn't want me to try. It probably wouldn't be edible. My assistant dropped off pizza."

I took one of the plates from his hand, and grabbed a couple of napkins. The tantalizing aroma hit me almost immediately. "God, I've missed pizza."

"You don't eat it?"

I shook my head. "Not usually. My body doesn't like carbs, even though I do. I love pizza, but I don't have it often."

He took his place on the couch. "But you're going to eat it, right?"

I inhaled again, my eyes already devouring what I knew was an amazing pie. It had come from one of the best pizzerias in or near downtown. "Yes," I said with a sigh.

I picked up a still-warm piece, my mouth watering. After another long sniff, I opened my mouth and let myself take a bite of the forbidden food. I couldn't help the small moan of pleasure I let out as the Italian flavor exploded in my mouth.

"This is amazing," I told him as soon as I swallowed.

Carter had already started on his second piece, but he was watching me as he devoured it.

We ate in silence for a few minutes: me savoring my food, and Carter wolfing his down.

Once I'd downed the second piece, I put the plate aside, even though he'd heaped it full. "I'm done. I have to control myself."

"Why?" he asked.

"I love food," I explained. "But I have to keep fitting into my current size for my job."

"I'll never understand why models have to be so damn thin," he grumbled.

"By modeling standards, I'm not thin," I informed him. "I'm actually bigger than most, so I stay fit. At one time, I was two sizes smaller. But I got tired of starving myself to death. So I decided I needed to get to a healthy weight and stay there. And if my clients refused to accept that, I'd just leave the modeling field altogether. Luckily, they didn't drop me. But I have to watch it."

I was a very healthy size six, and my body felt like my own now that I wasn't trying to be what the industry wanted me to be.

"I doubt a little pizza is going to make a difference," he observed. "Hell, I'd rather work out more than give up my cream cheese dogs."

I wrinkled my nose. "You actually eat those? They're disgusting."

In my opinion, cream cheese and hot dogs didn't mix, and I'd never understood why people in Seattle ate them.

He dropped his napkin on his now empty plate. "Have you tried them?"

I shook my head.

"Don't knock them until you've actually tried them," he advised as he stood. "They're as addictive as Dick's cheeseburgers."

I smiled at him. "Eat a lot of junk food?"

"All the time," he confessed. "I like to eat."

If he didn't work out so much, I had no doubt that Carter would be sporting a belly.

But he didn't have an ounce of fat on his body, which I found completely unfair since he ate anything he wanted. He was all ripped and toned muscle.

He took my plate into the kitchen, and returned a few minutes later.

As he took his seat again, I said, "I owe you, Carter. Thanks for taking care of me today."

"You don't owe me shit," he argued. "I kissed you in an elevator, remember?"

"That's a little bit different than hanging out with me all day, and making sure that I'm doing okay."

"So you feel indebted?"

"I do, and it's not something I'm used to."

"Get used to it," he advised in a low baritone. "I plan on hanging out as long as you're not able to get around. And if you're worried about owing me, I could think of plenty of ways you can pay me back."

His eyes were tumultuous as he stared at me, the intensity of his gaze startling.

I had a feeling that we weren't talking about a future casual friendship.

With Carter, I was pretty sure nothing was going to be simple.

And I had no idea how I felt about that.

Chapter 8

Brynn

"Carter is driving me crazy," I shared with Laura while we were having coffee four days after my injury. "I can't walk across my condo without tripping over him."

She raised an eyebrow as she sat next to me at my little kitchen table. "And that's really a bad thing? There are plenty of women who'd love to have a man like him camped out at their house."

I hadn't slept all that well the night before, so I was crabby. "I don't want him around that much. I'm used to being independent."

"You were injured, Brynn. He's just trying to help. Actually, I'm starting to like him. He might be an alpha male, but I think it's pretty sweet that he's been here for you when you needed some help."

Laura and Carter had bumped into each other several times during the last several days, and I'd noticed that my friend was starting to warm to the man who seemed to know I needed things before I did.

"He feels guilty," I informed her. "He feels like he caused the whole accident, even though I was the one not paying attention."

Laura set her mug down on the table and swallowed a mouthful of coffee before she said, "I highly doubt that's the only reason he's been hanging around. He obviously likes you."

And *that* was the problem. I was pretty sure Carter *did* like me. And I didn't understand him at all. There were scores of women who would be at his beck and call if he wanted, so why spend time with a female who wouldn't?

"I don't want to like him," I admitted grudgingly.

She gave me that look, the one that reminded me of something a big sister would give her younger sibling. "Because of your past? Brynn, you can't let your past define who you are now. It wasn't your fault."

I definitely didn't want to talk about that, so I replied, "I don't need a relationship, Laura. I'm too busy. I still need to travel, and we have the future business to think about."

She sighed. "I think you'd like a relationship, but you're afraid. It's funny that I really want one myself, but I've never met the right guy. And I really want to have kids. I've always wanted them."

"Are you still thinking about using a sperm donor? Laura, you have time—"

"I'm just *thinking* about it and getting a consult," she said, holding up her hand defensively. "But the more I consider it, the better it sounds."

Maybe I wasn't interested in finding a permanent guy, but I wanted Laura to have one. She deserved someone to cherish her and any children that she had. "Just wait a little longer. Maybe you'll meet somebody."

She snorted. "I've been saying that for years, and I'd like to still be young enough to have fun with my kids. But this isn't about me right now, Brynn. It's about you, and a guy who might really like you, somebody you could end up caring about."

I rolled my eyes. "I barely know him."

"But he gets to you."

"He's attractive. It's lust, Laura. Who wouldn't want to get Carter Lawson into their bed?"

I shuddered even thinking about the reaction that my body always had every time I was close to Carter.

Laura shrugged. "Then sleep with him and find out if he's really a sexy stud."

The problem was, I *did* want to explore the insatiable lust I felt every time I saw him, but something told me that Carter Lawson was different. He wouldn't be a one-nighter. At least, not for me. I had a feeling he'd be hard to forget. And even though I didn't want to admit it, the way he affected me made me uneasy.

There was something about him that I connected with, and it wasn't just his hot body and ridiculously handsome face.

Sometimes, Carter looked…haunted during his occasional unguarded moments, and against my better judgment, I really wanted to know why.

Finally, I shook my head. "Forget it." I wasn't sure whether I was talking to myself or to my best friend. "I'm recovered, and my ankle is okay, so we probably won't see each other much."

Although I wouldn't trust my injured leg with another jog right now, the swelling was pretty much gone, and I could walk without limping. Carter hadn't shown up early this morning, so he obviously knew I could take care of myself now.

"I wouldn't count on him not hanging around anymore. I've seen the way he looks at you," Laura answered.

"How does he look at me?"

She laughed. "Like a guy who's desperate and determined to get what he wants. He's not giving up, Brynn. Count on it."

I frowned at Laura, hoping she was wrong. If Carter were to hang out at my place any longer, I'd find myself pretty tempted to take her advice and sleep with him just to see if the ache I experienced every single time he was near me would just go away.

Honestly, it was getting unbearable.

I'd never responded to a man the way I did to Carter.

He didn't even have to touch me to make me want him with an intensity I'd never experienced before.

Because I didn't want to think about Carter Lawson, I changed the subject. "How are things going at the store?"

Laura smiled. "Amazingly well. But we're going to have to scale up production soon. We're selling things almost as fast as we're making them. It's been really busy."

Our costs were high because our production numbers were small with just one shop. It would reduce our costs to produce a higher quantity. "Then let's do it. Now that we know what items are selling hot, we can up the amounts produced on those items."

Laura leaned back in her chair and folded her arms. "I really think you should think about producing your ideas for the handbags. They're brilliant. You could do your own thing. They don't have to be manufactured for our brand. You can make them your own."

I'd worked on various designs for my purses, and I'd just shown Laura some of them before we'd sat down for coffee. "You don't think they'd fly at the store?"

She shrugged. "I have no idea if they would or wouldn't, and I'm very willing to try them there. But because your ideas are more specialized for travel, I think you should make your own brand for them."

The more I worked on the designs, the more determined I was to make the perfect bag for a woman who travels. Having been the victim of more than one purse snatching while I was abroad, I really wanted to make the perfect line of travel bags. One that actually made sense.

"It was just an idea," I explained. "And I need to work on more designs for the store."

"I can handle that," she said. "I'll just run the stuff by you before I put them into production. I have more items than we can possibly produce right now, Brynn, and I keep piling them up every single day."

I felt guilty about not contributing to our design portfolio as much as Laura did, but my friend was a natural at producing new ideas for clothing every day. Truthfully, I was so much better at handbag designing than I was at developing fashionable attire.

Was it possible that I really could eventually start my own line of purses?

"Maybe I should just step out of Perfect Harmony," I considered. "This has always been your baby, and you started the store. I love the line, but it's more yours than mine."

It was possible that I'd gotten caught up in the idea and the excitement. And while I was perfectly capable of doing an adequate job at designing clothing, I wasn't nearly as good at it as Laura.

She lifted an eyebrow. "Is that what you want? Truly, Brynn, I won't be mad if you want to go in your own direction. But I won't be able to pay you back your investment right now."

I shook my head. "Don't worry about that. Maybe I can just be an investor. I know a great startup company when I see it. And I know the company is going to thrive."

I didn't need the money I'd put into Perfect Harmony, and I honestly knew it was going to be enormous someday. The world needed a company that embraced body diversity, and a designer like Laura who could create styles that would flatter most women.

She nodded. "We'll work it out. And I'd love to see you working on something that's really your passion."

"I'll still help you out," I vowed. "Carter offered to help me with marketing the brand, and giving advice on scaling up when you're ready."

Laura let out a low whistle. "What I wouldn't give to have a marketing genius like him in my corner."

"Then I'll take him up on his offer."

She beamed. "Thanks. I'm grateful for any input or ideas. Marketing isn't my strong point."

"I hope it won't strain your finances if I drop out of the partnership," I said sincerely. The last thing I wanted was to cause Laura stress.

"I'll be fine," she reassured me. "I have the funds, and I've been thinking about launching online. Now that I have the flagship store, maybe I could make everything more internet-based. I know what sells, and if I had the right marketing, I think I could make a go of it on the web."

"That's brilliant," I said excitedly.

Laura and I both had an enormous following on social media, and she had a lot of friends who had big audiences.

"I'd have to do more research, but I really think this is a business that needs to be on the internet."

"You know I'll help you in any way I can," I said softly. "It's not like I'm going to dump the company altogether. I just think it really should be yours."

"You know I'm going to hound you until you get your own brand going," she warned.

I smiled. "I know."

When my best friend wanted me to do something she thought would be good for me, she was tenacious. It was a trait that I both admired and hated.

"I'll work on it," I promised.

"You know, you could move back to Michigan. Now you really have no reason to stay in Seattle except me," she said. "But I'm selfishly hoping you won't go."

"Not a chance," I said adamantly. "I've come to love this city. Besides, you need me. I'll still be an investor, and I have to convince Carter to help with a marketing plan."

I didn't mention that the last thing I wanted was to move back to my hometown. I'd used the excuse of needing to be in the city so Laura and I could launch our shop, but deep down inside, I realized that I couldn't go back permanently. The memories would haunt me.

"Thank God," she answered with a sigh. "I don't know what I'd do if you were that far away."

"I'm not going anywhere," I assured her. "But I am booking a trip to see my mom. She's seeing someone, and I want to talk to her."

"She has a man in her life?" she questioned. "I think that's fantastic."

"I don't," I replied flatly. "What if he's not everything he seems to be?"

"What if he is?" she questioned. "What if he's amazing, and he makes her happy?"

"Then I have to see it with my own eyes," I told her.

"When are you going?"

"I'm not sure. I'll book my flight this afternoon."

"Don't judge the poor guy because of your history," she said in a soft, soothing voice. "I know you're wary about men in general, but he could be the best thing that ever happened to your mom."

It was hard not to let my past color my judgment. "I'll try to be fair."

"Is she still trying to get you to date more?"

I laughed. "When *doesn't* she try to get me married off so I can provide her with grandchildren?"

"Never," Laura said. "But I think she just wants you to be happy and finally heal."

Laura had met my mother a couple of times over the years when I'd dragged her along for my holiday visits back home, and she'd experienced the pressure my parent could exert.

"I am happy," I said. "I don't need a man to complete me."

"No," she agreed. "But it would be nice to find that guy who makes you even happier than you are now."

I contemplated Laura's words as she got up and took her mug to the dishwasher.

Was there any man who could ever make me feel like my love for him was more important than my fear?

Sadly, I was pretty certain that the answer to that question would always be *no*.

And for the life of me, I couldn't figure out why that fact troubled me more now than it ever had in the past.

I'd always been happier alone.

Now, even though I knew I wasn't capable of loving a man that much, the whole idea of spending my life solo was more than slightly depressing.

Brynn

"What in the hell am I doing!" I said to myself as I tossed the lipstick I'd been applying onto the vanity with disgust.

After not hearing from Carter the entire day, he'd finally called a half hour ago. Against my better judgment, I'd accepted his invitation to come see his penthouse.

I'd showered.

I'd fussed with my hair.

I'd put on a pretty sundress.

And on top of all that, I was putting on makeup like I was getting ready to do a cover shoot.

Enough! I don't plan on being in Carter's penthouse for more than ten minutes.

Even though I hated to admit it, I was nervous.

I'd been okay when I was physically incapacitated, but now that I was going to his place healthy, it was kind of nerve-racking.

Yeah, he'd asked me how I was getting around, and there had been concern in his voice, but after that, his low baritone had been full of sin, promised pleasure, and so many other things that made me edgy.

I'm going to thank him for what he did for me. That's all.

I heard my doorbell ring as I was exiting my bedroom, and I knew exactly who it was.

Carter had to come get me since I couldn't get to the penthouse without a card key.

I tried to shrug off the electric tingle that slithered up my spine in anticipation.

This is not a date. This is not a date.

The mantra was still playing over and over in my brain as I opened the door.

The second I saw him, I knew I was in trouble.

Although he looked good in anything, he was wearing a gray, custom suit with a gorgeous navy-blue tie that matched his eyes.

"Hi," I said breathlessly.

"You look beautiful," he rasped, his voice sounding scratchy, like he was unused to giving a compliment.

And yeah, I'd gotten used to accepting compliments, but there was something about the way he looked at me, like he wanted to devour me whole, that felt so much different than any other flattery I'd ever received before.

"Thanks," I said automatically as I grabbed my purse, my heart thundering against my chest wall as I exited my condo and turned to lock the door.

I needed to stop acting like a giddy idiot.

This wasn't a date.

I couldn't ever be with a man like Carter Lawson.

The attraction between us was way too intense, but I had to learn to ignore it.

We were silent until we got to the private elevator. Once we stepped inside, I said, "I want to thank you for everything you did to help me while I couldn't get around."

"Did you really think I'd abandon you after I'd slammed you to the ground?" he asked, sounding slightly disappointed.

"I'm not sure what I expected," I shared honestly. "But I guess I never expected you to be so…nice."

He shrugged as he put the keycard in to make the elevator climb. "Guess I can't blame you. I'm not exactly known for being considerate."

He said the words like it was just a fact.

I leaned back and crossed my arms. "Why?"

"I'm a businessman, Brynn. And I'm good at what I do. That generally means I have to be ruthless."

"Are you?"

"What?" he questioned.

"Are you ruthless?"

"When I have to be," he countered.

For some reason, I didn't think he was a jerk all the time. In fact, I'd experienced the more amiable side of him for the last several days, so I knew for a fact that he could be genuinely nice. "I think there's a soft spot inside the cutthroat businessman," I observed.

Generally, I would never get personal with a guy I'd only known for a short period of time, but there was something about Carter that made me want to figure him out.

He was an enigma. I knew he could be brutal in business, but I didn't buy that it was anything more than a performance for him.

Carter was definitely used to getting his way, but he was still empathetic. Maybe he wasn't very good at showing it sometimes, but I had a feeling he wasn't completely narcissistic.

As usual, he looked composed, sophisticated, and completely in control.

He leaned back as we climbed to the penthouse, giving me a dangerous look. "Don't count on finding something good inside me," he drawled. "It doesn't exist."

"Everybody has a weakness," I mused. "What's yours? Your family?"

There had to be something that broke him down, something that made him more human.

The elevator bell dinged as we hit the top of the building.

"Right now, that *weakness* appears to be you," he answered as the doors swung open, and he didn't sound happy about it.

Honestly, I understood his reluctance to admit he had any vulnerability. I didn't like having an Achilles' heel either.

The elevator doors *whooshed* closed, leaving us in a small space that led to his penthouse.

"Do you want a drink?" he asked after he'd unlocked the door and we stepped inside.

"White wine if you have it," I murmured distractedly as I surveyed his home.

The floor-to-ceiling windows made for a breathtaking view, and I walked to them without thinking about it. "You have an amazing vantage point here," I told him as I gazed down at the sweeping views of the city lights. "And I thought *my* condo had fantastic views."

I finally turned to find Carter at the bar, making drinks.

"Feel free to look around," he offered.

"I'm pretty sure I might get lost," I mumbled.

He looked up and shot me a grin. "Don't worry. I'll find you."

Since he'd offered, I wandered into the kitchen, which was positively enormous. A chef's kitchen that had me dumbfounded. What guy who didn't cook needed one this damn big? The monstrous island was over the top.

"I thought you didn't cook," I called out to him.

"I don't."

"That's a shame," I said in a voice he couldn't possibly hear as I continued my journey, discovering that he had a private gym that could put professional ones to shame, an indoor pool and spa, a media room, and a library I'd love to have—all on the first floor of his home.

I let out a sigh as I touched the leather spines on a beautiful set of Harvard Classics, and an Easton Press collection that made me envious.

Strangely, everything in the home was contemporary, a style I actually loved. But he seemed to have eclectic tastes when it came to reading. There was sci-fi next to the classics, and he seemed to have a lot of history books.

I strolled out of the library after I'd gotten over the fact that Carter apparently loved to read.

Moving back out to the open living space, I passed him as I moved up a spiral staircase to see the second floor.

Every bedroom had an en suite bathroom and a sitting area. But I was stunned when I finally hit the master.

I was accustomed to the nicer things, but Carter's room was completely decadent. Not only did it have a huge sitting area, but the entire room had the same floor-to-ceiling windows as the huge living area downstairs.

There was a breakfast area with a fridge and a breakfast table.

And his spa bathroom was gorgeous.

"Unbelievable," I uttered as I wandered out of the bathroom.

Carter wasn't an ostentatious type of guy. He obviously liked the contemporary style that was no-nonsense. The house had clean lines, vaulted ceilings, and not a single hint of gold or fancy, ornate light fixtures.

That was probably why I loved his home so much. I favored the same type of designs.

Sure, some of his abstract art pieces and sculptures were probably pricey, but the décor was far from being gaudy.

In a short amount of time, I discovered his home office, and I couldn't resist going in to take a look.

I was taken aback when I saw the personal pictures adorning a large amount of wall space.

"Do you need rescue, or can you find your way back downstairs?" I heard Carter drawl from the open office door.

I smiled. I couldn't help myself. "I think I'll be fine. I was just looking at your pictures. You played college football?"

He had a section dedicated to his college years, and most of them were of him in football gear.

"I did. I was one of the few Ivy League players whose stats were good enough to get drafted into the NFL."

"What happened?" I asked curiously.

"I wanted to go on with my education. I loved the game, and I still do. But it wasn't real life for me. I wanted something...different. I guess I just didn't have enough passion for it to get my brains scrambled as an adult."

I turned to look at him. He'd moved in right behind me, studying the photos himself.

Interesting. He'd turned down the chance to be a football superstar to keep studying.

I grilled him on some of the other photos. Finally, I asked about a family picture that looked like it had been taken while Carter was still in college.

"Is that your parents and your sisters?" I asked, pointing at the large photo.

I recognized the Lawson brothers, but I'd never seen much about his sisters.

I thought I'd seen a moment of sadness flash in his eyes as he pointed to the two young women. "This is Harper, and this one is Dani. And yeah, those are my parents in the back. They died in a car accident. They were hit by a drunk driver just as I was finishing my graduate degree."

My heart ached for him. It was pretty evident that he still wasn't over his loss. "I'm so sorry," I answered softly.

"Don't be," he said gruffly. "It was my damn fault."

Before I could answer, Carter turned and left the room.

Chapter 10

Brynn

I followed Carter downstairs, still reeling from his statement that he'd somehow caused his parents' deaths.

I took the glass of wine he offered, and we both sat in the spacious living room. I sat in a comfy chair, and Carter sat across from me on the sofa.

"If your parents were hit by a drunk driver, how were you in any way at fault?" I asked.

Maybe I shouldn't pry, but I'd seen the brief, haunted look on his face, and I couldn't let it go.

"Just forget it," he said in a raspy voice. "I'm not even sure why I said it."

He obviously believed it, so I didn't want to forget it. "Tell me," I prodded. I was the last one who was going to judge him.

There was a long silence before he spoke. "I was home on break from college. Two days after I got there, I came down with a cold. Mom was being Mom, and she decided she needed to go get some medicine because she didn't have anything in the house. My dad decided to ride along with her. Fifteen minutes later, they were both gone. Because I had a goddamn cold."

"Carter, she was your mother. Mine would have done the same thing. It was the drunk driver's fault, not yours." I was flabbergasted that he'd shouldered the blame.

"Why in the fuck did I even mention the fact that I was feeling like shit to them? The fact is, had I not been at home and whining about being sick, they'd still be here."

"You can't do this to yourself, Carter. You can't. Things just happen. Everyone who dies an untimely death was in the wrong place at the wrong time. You'll drive yourself crazy if you keep blaming yourself. Certainly none of your siblings think you're responsible."

"They don't know," he replied, his voice raw. "I never mentioned why they were out, and I was the first one to get home on break."

"I don't honestly think any of them would blame you. It wouldn't make sense. You need to stop thinking it's your fault. I have a feeling your parents would hate it that you did and still do."

God, I could feel his pain, and it was tearing me apart. I understood how his mind could go to those dark places, but it had to stop.

"Fuck, don't you think I know that?" he rasped. "But I've never been able to stop thinking about how things could have gone differently that day if *I'd* just done something different."

"I get that. I really do," I said emphatically. "It's easy to blame ourselves for something that had absolutely nothing to do with our actions. But in truth, it was a drunk driver who killed your parents, not you. Your actions were innocent. You were sick. It was out of your control. And your mother would have noticed even if you hadn't mentioned it. Mothers are scary that way."

"Yeah, my mom noticed everything," he conceded. "I think she had eyes in the back of her head."

"I understand that you miss them," I said gently. "But they wouldn't want you to eat yourself alive over something that's not your fault."

He caught my gaze, and I felt submerged in his pain. I hurt because I understood him.

"I'll try," he said in a clipped tone, his eyes now shuttered and wary. He tossed back half of his drink, and I sipped mine.

I knew he'd just brought the subject to an abrupt close. Carter Lawson wasn't the type of guy who wanted to be in any way vulnerable, and I knew I'd just gotten a rare glimpse at his soul.

But he wasn't about to keep baring it to me.

"So how is the clothing business going?" he asked, sounding completely composed again.

"I decided to become a silent investor instead of a partner," I shared. "I have other things I want to pursue, but I'll still be there for Laura whenever she needs me. And I'd love to get any advice you have for marketing."

"What made you decide to do that?" he asked curiously.

"It was actually Laura's passion, not mine. I love the entire concept, and I believe in it, but I decided I'd rather design travel bags. I've always had a frustration with purses. It's a problem I'd like to solve. I'm determined to make a bag that makes sense."

"Not that I know a damn thing about handbags, but why don't they make sense now?"

I picked up the purse I was using. "This. It's a designer bag that's really stylish, but I hate it. I've pretty much hated every purse I've ever had." I tipped it toward him. "What sense does it make to have two open pockets? I pretty much never use them. If I'm traveling, everything has to go into the zipper part because if I dump it over, everything falls out. And don't get me started on the fact that it isn't practical if I'm traveling to a rainy area. It's not weather resistant."

He lifted a brow. "I have a feeling there's more."

I sighed. "I travel, and I've had my purse snatched three times, and been pickpocketed a few more times. Twice, the thief cut the strap. To be practical for traveling, the bags would need an indestructible cross body strap, and a wallet with RFID security to keep my credit card numbers from being stolen."

He grinned. "Anything else?"

"Yes. It still needs to be stylish. Why can't function be pretty? I want it all. There are some decent travel bags now, but I want one that has everything."

"Then I guess you'll have to do it yourself. Business is all about wanting more," he contemplated. "That's why Lawson did so well. My brothers and I wanted it all, too. You can do this, Brynn. Go for what you want. And don't settle for anything less."

"I'm working on it," I confided. "I want to do a whole line of gorgeous travel bags that women can travel with safely."

"Can I see it?" he asked. "I'm still willing to help you out in any way I can with either one of your businesses."

I shook my head. "I'm not done with it yet. I still have a lot of research to do, and I have to finish the designs. I'm hoping to have a trial version as soon as possible so I can test it when I travel for my shoots."

"When do you have to go?"

"I need to go see my mom. It's been way too long, and I'm going to book my trip to Michigan. I don't have to travel for business for a few months."

"You don't have to book a flight," he said. "I have a private jet that will take you anywhere you want to go."

I looked at him, stunned. "I can't just use your private jet. It's expensive."

"I think I can handle the added expense," he said wryly. "And if I'm not using it, it just sits at the hangar. When did you plan on going to Michigan?"

I shrugged. "Probably in a couple of weeks."

"Give me a date and I'll take care of it."

I had to admit, accepting his offer was tempting. I'd have to do one or two layovers to get to Michigan, and going direct would be so nice. But there was no way I was using Carter's jet. "We'll see," I answered noncommittally.

"You said you wanted to thank me for helping you out. Take my jet and we'll call it even."

I let out a startled laugh. "I don't think that accepting another favor is actually a thank-you."

"It could be," he answered.

I held up a hand in defeat. "Okay. Let me think about it."

"Is it always this hard to get you to accept an offer to help you out?" he asked.

I thought about his question for a moment before I answered. "Other than my mom and Laura, nobody has ever really offered to help me. I had to fight hard to get to the top of my field. And then I taught myself to become a good investor since I know I won't be a model forever. I've pretty much been on my own since I was a teenager. My mom had cancer, so it was time for *me* to take care of *her*. I didn't want to bother her with any of my issues. They were pretty small compared to hers."

"What about your dad?"

"He's been out of my life since I was fourteen, and he's dead now," I told him.

"No siblings?"

I shook my head. "None. But Laura has been like a sister to me. We met pretty early in our careers. We both decided that we weren't going to compromise our health for a modeling career, and we've stuck with that together ever since."

"What about boyfriends? None of them ever offered?"

His question was stilted and tense, like he didn't really want to hear about my love life.

"I don't have complicated relationships, Carter. I can't. I travel too much."

He shrugged. "I don't do complicated either, so I get that."

I downed the rest of my wine, and then stood up. I knew I needed to leave, but strangely, I didn't really want to go. "I better get back down to my condo."

He stood. "Have dinner with me, Brynn. I know I was kind of a jerk last time I asked, but this time I'm asking because I'd really like to spend time with you."

I gave him my empty wine glass as he held his hand out for it, shocked by how much I really wanted to say yes. I didn't want the night to end, either, but I was starting to like Carter way too much.

He wasn't nearly as arrogant as he'd come off on first acquaintance. He hid the good parts of himself well, but there was a decent man beneath his alpha arrogance. I just didn't know if I wanted to know all of him.

It would make the lust I had for him even worse.

I followed him to the kitchen, where he was putting our glasses in the dishwasher. "I can't, Carter. I'm sorry."

He turned to face me. "I don't get you, Brynn. I think we both know that we have some kind of crazy chemistry. I think we need to explore it. You feel it, too. I know you do."

I nodded slowly. "I'm not even going to try to deny that. I'm attracted to you, Carter. But I just told you that I don't do complicated."

His expression was intense as he answered in a graveled voice, "It doesn't have to be complicated. We just need to figure out what's happening, because I've sure as hell not wanted a woman as much as I want you. Hell, this isn't comfortable for me, either. But I can't just fucking ignore it."

"You have women falling at your feet," I squeaked. "You don't need me."

He moved forward like a predator stalking his prey. "I think I *do* need you, Brynn."

He was close, so close that I could feel the heat radiating from his body, and it set mine on fire. I wanted this man so much that I ached, but he scared me.

I was backed up to the counter, and I stared up at him. He made me feel safe and terrified at the same time.

His first touch was gentle, just a thumb on my cheek that trailed gently down my face.

"I want to kiss you, Brynn, but I promised I'd ask for your permission. Don't say no," he said huskily, his blue eyes drilling into mine.

My body was trembling just from a simple touch. What would it be like if I let him kiss me again?

"Carter," I whispered, feeling like I was in a lust-filled trance.

He put a hand into my hair, but he was gentle, his fingers merely exploring. "I need to kiss you," he said gutturally.

My damn body was betraying me, and I wanted to make a connection with Carter so desperately that it was getting physically painful.

I could feel his warm breath on my lips, but it was obvious that he wasn't going to close the small distance without me saying the one word that would make it happen.

All I had to do was say the word.

"Yes," I said in a voice that was almost a moan.

I reached up, sank my hands into his hair, and yanked his mouth down to mine.

The moment our lips touched, I surrendered. Maybe it was just a brief encounter, but I was going to revel in it.

Because Carter liked control, I gave it to him. And got exactly what I needed.

He devoured my mouth, his tongue owning it. The chemistry between us ignited until I was giving back as much as he gave.

I whimpered as he lifted his head to nibble on my lips, and then swooped down again for more.

Sweet baby Jesus! I can't get enough.

There was nothing I wanted more than to rip open his shirt just so I could touch his bare skin.

In that moment, I was willing to give him every damn thing he wanted, and *that* was the thought that made me come to my senses.

I was panting when I finally pushed against him, needing to put some distance between us.

He lifted his head and looked at me, his expression puzzled. "What's wrong?" he asked hoarsely.

"I can't do this, Carter. I can't," I said, feeling panicked and breathless.

He gently pushed a stray hair away from my face. "Why, Brynn? Tell me what's wrong."

Tears of frustration started to trickle down my cheeks. I could easily give him some bullshit, but after what he'd shared earlier, I gave him the truth. "I have trust issues, Carter. Big ones. I have for a long time. I can't explain. I'm sorry. I need to go."

He leaned back, and I took the opportunity to wriggle out of his embrace.

Embarrassed, I scrambled to make my way to the front door, and was relieved when I was able to go down the elevator without a key.

Only when I was safely in my own condo could I lean back against the closed locked door and really cry.

Chapter 11

Carter

"Do you seriously believe that Mom and Dad died because you were sick?" Jett asked the next day, his voice astonished.

My little brother had wanted to take a break from all the party planning that his fiancée and her best friend were doing at his penthouse, so I'd met him at a bar by the waterfront for a drink.

Fuck! It seemed like once I'd spilled my guts to Brynn, I was determined to become a guy who actually talked about his emotions. I'd given up the whole story of how our parents had been out because of me to Jett.

I didn't like doing it, but I couldn't seem to help myself.

What in the hell was Brynn doing to me?

I didn't talk about heavy shit. *Ever.* Business was my life.

"Maybe not so much anymore," I confessed to Jett as we sat at an outside table, downing a couple of beers. "But it seems like every person I get close to either dies or gets hurt. I've never been any good for anybody."

"How do you figure?" Jett asked.

"What if I'd signed up with PRO to do the rescue missions you ended up doing? Marcus asked me to be part of it, and I turned him down. I was too damn busy trying to conquer the business world. Would you ever have signed up to risk your ass trying to get hostages out of hostile countries? And even if you did, would me being there have changed the way the helicopter accident happened? Could it have been me who got injured instead of you? Because I would have been fucking happy to have it be me instead of you."

My little brother looked stunned, and I couldn't really blame him. I was generally a cold-hearted bastard, but everything I'd just said was the truth.

There was a long silence before Jett answered. "I wouldn't have preferred it was you. Carter, nobody can protect us from some of the shitty things that happen in life. Yes, I would have still signed up even if you did, and nothing would have gone differently except you could have been killed or injured, too. Dude, you can't protect everybody you care about. Don't you think I would give anything to have protected Ruby from the nightmare life she had before she met me? Hell, I could convince myself that somehow, I could have met her earlier. You have to stop this shit. Bad things happen. And no matter how much we wish they didn't, we can't shoulder the blame for every crappy thing that happens to people we love."

"Why the fuck can't we protect them?" I rasped, right before I chugged down a large portion of my beer.

"Because if we spend all our time trying to prevent anything bad from happening, we aren't enjoying every moment we have with them. Because of Ruby's past, I was obsessed with protecting her. Sometimes I still am. But I was suffocating her. I had to back off and let life happen while doing my best to make sure she's okay. You have to trust the good judgment of the people you care about, and know that life is going to throw everybody some curveballs. You haven't been living, Carter. You've been too damn afraid that something else is going to happen. I think that's what motivated you when you tried to break up my relationship with Ruby, right?"

I nodded. Hell, I still hated myself for nearly depriving Jett of his happiness.

"Your actions were motivated by concern for me. That almost makes it possible for me to forgive you. It was highly misguided, but I know you love me," he said with a grin.

"Who said I love you?" I grumbled. "Maybe I just thought you were being stupid."

Jett let out a chuckle. "You do. But you need to stop thinking that anything you do is going to prevent unhappiness. I was willing to take a risk with Ruby. I'm a grown adult male. You should have respected that. And I was willing to take the chance that something could happen when I signed up with PRO. Believe it or not, I really don't regret it. I'd do it all over again to save the lives we saved while PRO was still in existence. We did good work. And I wouldn't have met or understood Ruby if things hadn't gone the way they did. I wouldn't trade being with her for anything."

I nodded. "That's because you're half crazy."

He shrugged. "Maybe. But I'm happy. Are you?"

I was a little surprised because nobody had ever asked me that question. I was a billionaire, I had my pick of women most of the time, and I had a company I was pretty damn proud to be a part of. "I'm not sure," I answered honestly.

"What happened with Brynn? You like her."

"She makes me crazy," I said unhappily. "She said she has trust issues."

I didn't want to share the really private moments I'd had with her, so I left it at that.

"Do you know why?" he queried.

I shook my head. "Another guy? Maybe somebody hurt her."

Just the thought of some bastard making Brynn unhappy didn't set well with me.

Jett leaned back in his chair. "Carter, you're all about protecting everyone. Make her understand the man you really are and not the prick you can be sometimes. She can get over trust issues. God knows that Ruby did. But it takes time."

"How did she get over it? Why does she trust you now?" I had to admit that Ruby had every reason not to trust one damn soul, yet she trusted Jett.

"She needed one person in her life who was never going to betray her. I gave her that."

"How?"

"You won't like the answer, but I had to make myself vulnerable to her. I had to be constant. I had to be there for her. And I wanted to be there."

"I want to be there for Brynn. But I want her so goddamn much that it's clouding my judgment. I don't get our connection. I don't get the emotional crap and the irrational behavior I seem to experience whenever I see her. It sucks."

"Make it work to your advantage," Jett suggested. "Maybe you won't always be rational, but you'll be there. Trust issues mean that person needs somebody stable. Somebody they can count on. Let her know you're not going anywhere, no matter how bad things get."

I looked at him warily. "You know that's not how I am."

He nodded. "Maybe you haven't been in the past. But you'll know if Brynn is somebody special if you can't stay away from her. I'm not saying to stalk her, but it sounds like she cares about you. If she didn't, she never would have revealed that kind of vulnerability to you."

I thought about his words for a minute. He was right. If she wasn't fighting the same attraction, would she have ever admitted that she had a vulnerability at all?

Nope.

She wouldn't.

On the surface, Brynn was independent and she had her shit together, with a great career. She'd invested herself to wealth instead of spending her money. And she was determined to make a future for herself when her modeling career wound down.

Fuck knew that she spoke her mind. And she was as smart as she was beautiful.

I think that's why I admired her so damn much.

I'd wanted to go after her when she'd left abruptly the night before, but I hadn't known what the fuck to say, or how to make things better. Maybe I should have followed my instincts and just been there, even if I didn't have the right words to make everything better.

I didn't know what was wrong, but I wanted to prove to her that I could be that guy she could count on, even if I was a prick sometimes.

But I'd been fighting the feeling that she'd be better off if I just left her alone.

"I think you might be right," I admitted reluctantly.

Jett smiled. "Damn! Did it hurt to say that?"

"You have no idea," I shot back.

He sobered. "If you want her, don't screw it up by thinking you're not good for her," he advised. "Start believing that you could be the only guy who can reach her if she has trust issues. You know if there's something there, Carter. I can't explain it, but you just know she's different from any woman you've ever met before."

"She has been from day one," I rumbled. "I knew she was beautiful because I'd seen her before, but the first time she smiled at me, I was pretty much screwed. She doesn't treat me like a billionaire. There's no way she was going to fall all over me just because I was rich. She has her own money. And she has no problem telling me off."

"I think I'd like to see that."

"Not happening." I loved bursting Jett's bubble when he was being an asshole.

"Why don't you bring her to the engagement party? I know Ruby would love to meet her. She follows her and Laura on social media. She likes their styles."

I liked Brynn's style, too. Probably more than I should. "We'll see. I'm not sure she's ever going to speak to me again."

"If you want her, you're going to have to work for her, Carter."

"I've never had to work to have a woman in my life." I wasn't being arrogant. It was just the truth, and I didn't know how to really romance a female. I only knew how to get them into my bed, and it generally wasn't all that hard.

Jett grinned. "You'll learn. Follow your instincts. And try to bring her to the party. I'm sure Ruby will sing your praises."

"At least I have an ally."

"You have a whole family of allies," he corrected. "You've just never realized it. All jokes aside, I fucking want you and Mason to find the same happiness that me, Harper, and Dani have now. Had I realized you, in any way, blamed yourself for losing Mom and Dad, I would have knocked you alongside the head for having those crazy thoughts. And I can guarantee you that so would Mason, Harper, and Danica."

"It's Brynn's fault I'm even talking about it," I shared. "For some reason, I'm a damn fountain of truth around her. I can't lie to her."

"Keep being honest. Sounds like she needs that," Jett said.

"I'll work on it," I told him truthfully as we both stood and tossed money on the table.

"I better get back," he said. "Thanks for the break."

I didn't feel the usual sense of guilt I experienced when Jett limped slightly beside me as we left the bar.

Instead of feeling like he was my wounded little brother, he was just…Jett. Always had been, really. He'd actually changed for the better after he'd met Ruby, and he was a hell of a lot happier than I was right now.

Lucky bastard!

Chapter 12

Brynn

"I'm not going anywhere," Carter growled as he barged through my front door. "I don't care if you have trust issues. You'll learn to trust me eventually."

I was dumbfounded, so befuddled that I just stood there at the open door as Carter paced in my living room.

After a moment, I closed the door, but I was still just staring at him.

I'd never planned on seeing him again after I'd sprinted from his penthouse like an idiot the night before. Not that I'd ever let anybody know I had an insecurity, but as far as I knew, it generally sent men scrambling to get away from a woman with *issues*.

He kept talking as he paced the living room.

"Maybe I *have* always blamed myself for shit that was really out of my control. Not that I like to think *anything* is out of my control," he rambled. "I'll be patient. Not that I've ever done *that*, either, but I'm fucking willing to try it if you just see this thing through with me until I figure out why the hell I can't stay away from you. Hell,

I'll even try not to touch you, but I sure as shit don't know if I can do that, either. But I can try so you'll trust me."

My heart felt like it was in a vise as I watched Carter Lawson, billionaire and powerful head of one of the world's biggest tech companies, trying to make me happy.

He was saying he was imperfect, and he couldn't have said anything more touching than that.

I pretty much crumbled in the face of his ranting.

Never in my life had I encountered a man like him, and probably never would again.

"I'm sorry about last night," I said as I moved forward to the living room, stopping right in front of him so he'd stop pacing.

"I don't care about that," he said in a guttural tone. "But I want you to be able to trust me. Maybe I've never really been the kind of guy most people trust, but I'd really like to try."

The fact that he was putting himself out there to me made me ache with a longing to let him get close. "I'm scared, Carter. I've never felt this way. Not ever. Sure, I've had sex. But I've never *wanted* someone this badly."

"Ditto," he grumbled. "So what are we going to do about it? Because I'm sure as hell not walking away this time. I can't."

"I don't think I can, either," I confessed with a sigh.

I'd cried for an hour after I'd come back from Carter's penthouse a complete mess. And I wasn't a woman who ever, ever cried, not even when I was by myself, much less in front of someone. I never gave any guy that kind of power over me. But for some reason, he rendered me nearly defenseless.

It was uncomfortable.

It was frightening.

But I couldn't blow off the way he made me feel and just walk away.

Carter Lawson was going to leave a scar regardless of what happened. The only question was how big of a wound it would be.

"So what do you want to do?" he demanded.

"Have dinner with you? It seems like a good place to start," I told him with a small smile.

He grinned, his demeanor completely changed. "I've never had to put my balls on a chopping block to get a woman to have dinner with me."

How could I explain that it was the fact that he *had* put himself out there that had made me feel okay about going out with him?

It didn't take a genius to figure out that everything Carter had said was foreign to him.

He was a powerful man, a guy who could pretty much get anything he wanted. A billionaire like him got everything *before* they even knew they needed it.

But he'd been willing to talk to me honestly.

Somehow, that made one of my walls tumble.

"You did get what you wanted," I pointed out.

"I want a hell of a lot more," he drawled. "But I can wait until your trust issues are resolved."

I shuddered as I looked into his eyes. I could feel the incendiary heat that was flowing between us from my scalp to my toes. My heart fluttered. Why could I not look at Carter without thinking about what all his intensity would be like if we were naked, our bodies entwined, and I could just completely immerse myself in all that passion?

I swallowed hard before I said, "Thank you."

He looked puzzled as he said, "For what?"

"For wanting to get to know me bad enough to be honest."

"Honesty sucks. But I'll get used to it," he countered.

I let out a startled laugh. "I'm sure you will."

Maybe he wasn't always sophisticated when he was being truthful, but I was even more convinced that there was so much more to this man than just the marketing genius of Lawson. I'd been sure of that since the beginning.

Carter Lawson wasn't comfortable with himself, but nobody understood that more than I did. He'd spent way too much time being the face of Lawson Technologies to really figure out that he was a pretty decent man.

"Do you want to talk about why you have trust issues?" he asked huskily.

I could see the concerned look in his eyes, but I wasn't ready to talk about my past. "Not yet. I was thinking more about dinner. I haven't eaten today."

"Pick your restaurant," he said agreeably.

Had I imagined the brief flicker of disappointment in his expression?

"Tonight, I'll cook," I told him. "But it won't be fancy."

"Do you like to cook?" he asked.

Carter had never seen me cook because I'd been ordered off my feet after my injury. "I love it. But I don't have everything I need to make something awesome."

"Anything is great if I don't have to cook it. But tomorrow, we're going out. Being with me isn't supposed to cause you more work."

"Come help me," I said, nudging him toward the kitchen.

"You'll be sorry you asked," he warned.

Turns out, his cautionary words were spot-on. I ended up sitting him down at my little kitchen table with a beer he'd gone to fetch from his penthouse after he'd almost taken off a finger trying to cut up some bell peppers.

He watched in apparent fascination as I cut up all the ingredients to toss into an omelet.

"How do you do that so fast?" he asked.

"Practice," I shared. "It was just me and my mom, and she worked a lot when I was a teenager. We shared cooking duties. When I went to New York to work on my own, I had to eat pretty healthy, and money was tight in the beginning."

"Did you really deprive yourself of food so you could model?" He didn't sound happy.

I started making the omelets as I said, "All the time. Modeling can be an ugly world. People think the life of a model is glamorous, but it's not. The day is pretty long when you're standing at a cattle call just to see if you can get a job, and the pay sucks if you don't have a name. And if you aren't naturally stick-thin, you pretty much starve to get into the standard tiny sizes. I was discovered at sixteen, but I was a late bloomer. Once I started developing hips and an ass, it was almost impossible for me to fit into a size two."

It was kind of amazing just how easy I could confide in Carter, but he made it comfortable by being so interested.

"So you didn't eat?"

"Sometimes I went without eating for days at a time, or basically lived on lettuce and water for a week. When I met Laura, we were both starting to get a name in the field. But we were both rundown and messing with our natural body types by trying to starve to keep working. Eating disorders are pretty common, and drugs to keep us thin weren't unusual. Laura was in worse shape than I was. What should have been her natural body type was bigger than mine, her bone structure is larger, and she was literally sick from starvation. I could see every bone through her skin. And I saw myself. That's when we decided that being a model for a decade wasn't worth risking health problems that would last a lifetime."

"So what did you do?"

I gave him a brief smile. "We got healthy. And said to hell with trying to fit into the sizes that designers wanted us to be. We both gained weight to get to our natural body type, and we exercised. Laura became a plus size model, the first one to grace the cover of popular women's magazines."

"She's not what I'd call plus size," Carter commented. "She's curvy."

"You'd be surprised what the industry considers plus size. They start even smaller than her. In the real world, it's not natural. And it isn't realistic. That's why we blog about body diversity. The average female size in the United States is a size fourteen. Yet models are still forced to fit into a size two. It's ridiculous. There are so few women who are actually that size naturally."

"I hate the thought of you going hungry," he rumbled.

"I don't anymore," I reassured him. "I'm my natural size, and I keep fit. If the day comes when that isn't enough to keep my jobs, then I'll bail out."

"You could bail out now," he suggested hopefully.

"I like what I do now," I said. "And Laura and I are constantly trying to send the message that women don't have to be something they aren't. They need to like themselves and accept themselves as they are."

"You'd be beautiful no matter what size you were," he said roughly.

My heart skipped a beat. There were so few people in my life who had not tried to make me something I wasn't. "Thanks. But enough about me. Tell me about your family. That was your older brother you were with at the charity gala, right?"

"Mason," he answered. "My older, workaholic, anal brother who I'm pretty sure hasn't gotten laid in at least a decade because he doesn't want to take the time out of the office. Jett is the youngest, he's engaged now, and I have two sisters who are married and living in our hometown of Rocky Springs, Colorado."

I flopped his veggie-filled omelet onto a plate, and added some potatoes I'd fried up for Carter, and then dropped a sweet roll onto a smaller plate. I set it in front of him as I said, "Do you see your sisters much?"

"Not often enough," he replied. "But they're coming for Jett's engagement party. It's been a while. I want to see my niece and nephew. Harper has two kids."

He dug into his food as I made my own omelet. I skipped the potatoes and the sweet roll, and joined him once my food was done.

"This is fantastic, Brynn. I don't think any woman has ever cooked for me."

I found that kind of sad, but I understood what he was saying: no female had ever seen him as anything except a guy who could take them to expensive restaurants. Honestly, because I was a supermodel who was supposed to live a glamorous life, no man had ever seen me as a normal female, either.

"I was happy to do it, and I'm not really into fancy places. I'm a foodie, but I'm more about the food than the ambiance. Some of the best places I've tried in Seattle are little hole-in-the-wall places that just make some incredible food."

He looked horrified. "Cheap restaurants?"

I nodded. "You should try them. And don't even try to tell me you're a food snob when you eat Dick's burgers, and cream cheese hot dogs."

He grinned as he placed his fork on his empty plate. "I did tell you that *you* could pick the restaurants."

"I'll be a pretty cheap date, Mr. Lawson," I joked.

He looked at me, his eyes glued to my face as he said huskily, "I don't give a damn where we go. All I care about is that *you are my date.*"

I kept eating, my heart light. There wasn't much I could say to a sweet comment like that.

Chapter 13

Brynn

The next few weeks were the happiest days I'd had in my entire life.

I spent the weekends doing things with Carter, and we spent the evenings discovering new places together.

We did the Space Needle, even though we'd both done it before.

We'd gone to art exhibitions, which were plentiful in Seattle.

Carter had taken me to explore the San Juan Islands, where we'd caught a whale-watching tour to watch the majestic Orca whales.

Since he'd offered, I definitely picked the restaurants for several days just to show him that *expensive* didn't necessarily mean *good* when it came to food.

Once I'd run out of favorite places, he took me to some of his. I had to admit, he had good taste. The pricey places were good, and we'd decided that we could live with doing a little of both, expensive and cheap, as long as the cuisine was flavorful.

We'd started working out together in his gym, or we'd go back to the park and take a run together.

Every single day, I discovered something new to like about Carter. His humor could definitely be dry and sarcastic, but so was mine, so he made me laugh.

I was getting way too used to being with a man who actually wanted to know me, and who seemed to care about whether or not I was happy. And I was way too accustomed to seeing his gorgeous face every day.

It was scary.

And it was addictive.

Maybe I should be running in the other direction because I craved him now, but I refused to let something special slip away just because of my fear.

Not once had Carter given me any reason to not trust him.

So I wasn't going to make him pay for my past.

He hadn't really touched me except to hold my hand, or slip an arm around my waist, and it was pure torture not to get him naked. But we'd enjoyed being together so much that I was willing to suffer if it meant we'd keep seeing each other.

But God, I really wanted to explore a more intimate relationship so badly that I could barely stand it.

"What are you thinking about?" he asked from across the table of a new Italian restaurant we'd decided to try.

"You," I murmured as I looked at the menu.

One thing I'd learned with Carter was that I could be completely honest and he never judged me.

"I hope you're picturing the two of us together naked," he teased.

Oh yeah, he never let up on the sexy comments. He just hadn't taken action on them.

"Actually, I was," I said in my best fuck-me voice. "I hope it was good for you, because it definitely was for me."

Everything was growing more intense between us, even our conversation. I think it was difficult because we'd fought the temptation for far too long.

"It would be more than good, Brynn," he answered in a hoarse voice.

I looked up at him. "I know."

My body literally trembled as our eyes met, and the force of our attraction hit me straight between my thighs. I was wet, and I was hungry. I could easily skip the food and go straight for Carter.

I nearly jumped out of my skin when the waiter interrupted our lustful cocoon to take our orders.

When our server had finally gone, Carter said, "I think I'm fucking losing it. I think I could have cleared the table and had sex with you right on this pretty white tablecloth."

I sucked in a sharp breath, my mind imagining what he'd just said.

I wanted to be naked and at Carter's mercy on the tablecloth, but... "I could do without everybody watching, but the rest certainly sounds enticing."

"You're right," he grunted. "I don't want any man to see you but me. Scratch that."

I heard my phone start to ring in my purse, and I turned to snatch it from my bag that was hanging from the chair.

"Hi, Mom," I said a little breathlessly. I'd seen who it was on the caller ID. "I'm out right now. Can I call you back from home?"

Carter had let his flight staff know that I'd be flying to see her next week or the week after, but I hadn't told *her* yet. I'd been pre-occupied and gone so much that we hadn't had a long conversation during the last few weeks.

"I have to tell you something, Brynn. Maybe I should have said something a long time ago. But I need to tell you now."

I was instantly alert because of her tone. My mother rarely sounded so nervous. "What's wrong? Is the cancer back?"

"No," she denied instantly. "It's not that. Nothing like that. Brynn, I finally did an interview about what happened. I knew you wouldn't agree, and I certainly wouldn't want to out you. But it's something I needed to do for closure."

"With who?" I said, feeling my stomach drop.

"Marissa Waters," she answered, her voice contrite.

"Oh, God." My hands began to shake, and I suddenly felt like I was going to vomit. Marissa Waters was an iconic female journalist, probably the best known in the country. "Why, Mom. Why do you need to talk about it?"

I'd spent years trying to live in the moment, to not think about the past or worry about the future. But my parent had *always* wanted to talk about what happened.

I...didn't.

"Because it's time," she said firmly. "It's the past, Brynn. We can't change it. I didn't mention you by name, and nobody is going to know who you are."

"I don't care about that," I argued. I wasn't that damn superficial. I was more concerned about the damage it could do to her emotionally. "I just really don't want to see you hurt."

"I think you hurt more than I do, baby girl," she answered. "I'm sorry if this upsets you, but the interview is playing tonight at nine. I wanted you to know before it aired."

"I don't want to see it," I said, alarmed.

Truth was, of course I was going to see it because she was my mother.

"You don't have to," she agreed. "I just didn't want you to see it without knowing. This is about me, Brynn, not you. I want to move on. I want to have something more with Mick in the future. And that means leaving the past in the past."

"I don't understand," I told her, my voice sounding whiney, even to my own ears. And I hated it.

"I'm sorry. Call me when you can," she requested. "I love you."

"I love you, too," I said automatically, but my emotions were raw.

I pushed the button to disconnect the call and dropped the phone on the table.

"Brynn, what the hell is wrong? You look like you've seen a ghost," Carter asked in a demanding voice.

"I'm fine," I denied.

Maybe I hadn't seen a ghost yet, but I was going to hear about one very shortly.

I glanced at my watch. It was an early dinner, so I'd be able to catch the interview when I got home.

"You aren't *fine*," he rasped as he grabbed my hand. "Your hands are cold, and you're shaking. Was that your mother?"

I looked at him and nodded. *What was he going to think if he knew the truth?*

"Something bad is going to happen, Carter."

"What?" he said in a powerful voice. "Tell me, Brynn. There's nothing we can't handle together."

I shook my head. "Not here. Not now. We'll talk when we get out of here."

"Then we're about to eat our fastest meal, because I don't like the way you're looking right now."

I took a deep breath and tried to focus on the moment.

I was here with Carter.

The past was the past.

I gave him a small, sad smile. "I'll live."

"Damn right you will. I'll make sure of it," he replied in a graveled voice.

I got through the meal, but Carter and I talked very little.

My past was getting ready to bite me in the ass, but it was finally time to tell somebody other than Laura the truth.

I just hoped Carter could really handle anything I threw at him, because my secret was monumental, and I wasn't sure I could deal with him walking away.

Chapter 14

Brynn

"Whatever it is, it doesn't matter," Carter growled as we walked into my condo.

I tossed my purse on the table and sat down on the couch. Usually, Carter took the chair beside me, but he plopped down right next to me.

I felt like a dam had burst inside me, and everything I was feeling needed to pour out.

I'd held my secret for a very long time, but I couldn't not share it with Carter anymore.

Things were way too intense, and too honest in our relationship.

I needed him right now. I needed to feel sane. I needed some kind of comfort, even though there really was none for what I was feeling.

"You don't know the truth yet," I said in a tremulous voice.

He turned to face me, his warm body so close that I just wanted to throw myself into his arms and let him tell me nothing mattered again.

But I couldn't.

"Then just tell me, Brynn. For fuck's sake, don't you know me well enough by now to figure out that I'm not going anywhere? I'm not going to judge you. Jesus! I've done some pretty shitty things in my life. There isn't much you can say that would be worse than what I've done."

I took a deep breath before I explained, "It isn't so much what I've done, but who I am."

He leaned back on the sofa. "I'm waiting. And I'll sit here all damn night until you explain what caused you to almost have a panic attack in the restaurant. And I know who you are. You're the female who's so damn beautiful, funny, and smart that you make me crazy."

Thank God he was stubborn, because I probably needed that right now.

I just wish I knew how to actually make the words come out of my mouth.

"My birth name wasn't Davis. I took my mother's maiden name when she changed hers back when I was fourteen," I explained in a whisper that was barely audible. "I was born Brynn Dixon. My father was Harvey Dixon."

He grasped my hand. "I don't understand. Who is Harvey Dixon?"

Obviously, the name didn't ring a bell for him, and I was almost relieved. But then I remembered that I'd still have to explain. "He was the Cross Country Killer, one of the most prolific serial rapists and killers in US history," I blurted out before I could change my mind.

He looked genuinely shocked.

I added, "I lived with a monster for fourteen years, and never knew. All I knew was that he was my dad. I loved him. He was a truck driver, and I couldn't wait until he got home from his runs. He taught me how to hit a softball, ride a bike, and I thought he loved me, but I found everything I knew about the father I loved was all a lie when the police came to arrest him. He'd raped scores of women and dumped their bodies. Some of them were only a few years older than me at the time. Minors who had no choice but to sell their bodies to stay alive."

I started to sob as the pain that was slicing through my heart became unbearable.

I'd been so confused.

So devastated.

And so damn lost.

And everything I'd felt at the age of fourteen came rushing back to me.

The only man I'd ever counted on as a child had been a completely different person from the father I knew.

Carter grabbed my upper arms and shook me gently. "Brynn, you're not your father."

"No, but I'm the daughter of a monster," I choked out, and then threw myself into his arms because I couldn't calm myself down.

They wrapped around me like steel, and I savored the feeling of being protected for once in my life.

"Shhh...Brynn. It really doesn't matter, sweetheart. That's his shame, not yours."

"I was fourteen years old. I felt betrayed," I told him on a strangled sob.

"Of course you did. Did your mom know? Did she have any hint of what was going on? If he killed that many women, it must have been happening for years."

I shook my head. "No. Neither of us knew. He provided. He came home and did the normal things a father does when he wasn't working. We went wherever I wanted to go. Until I became a teenager, he tucked me into bed at night with a story. When we first found out, I defended him because he was my father. I thought the police had to have the wrong man, right? But I was the one who was wrong, and when Mom and I saw the evidence, we knew the truth."

"God, I'm so damn sorry, Brynn." Carter tightened his arms around me.

I continued talking because I couldn't stop. "People blamed me and Mom. They said we could have stopped him. That we should have noticed something. My friends weren't allowed to talk to me anymore. We were isolated from our community, became the enemy even though Mom and I didn't know and had nothing to do with it."

"So that's why she changed your name?" he asked, his voice angry.

"Changed our names and moved us across Michigan, and I started in a new school. It was a secret. I couldn't tell anyone. Nobody knew that I was secretly wondering if I was like him."

"Stop, Brynn," he demanded. "You're not guilty by association, and you were the victim, not the killer."

"I feel guilty. I always have."

"Christ! Nobody knows that feeling more than I do, but you know it's not true."

I pulled back slowly from him so I could look him in the eyes. All I saw was compassion and anger, and I knew he wasn't pissed off at me. "I went to counseling for years. Rationally, I know that I wasn't to blame, Carter. But I can't shake the fact that my father was a serial murderer. And maybe we missed something. He was killing for well over a decade. And it still creeps me out that he used to hold me like a loving father holds their child."

"Listen to me, sweetheart. This. Was. Not. Your. Fault." His voice was graveled and agitated, but there was comfort there, too.

"I think I've spent my life running away because I was terrified that *everybody* would be different. That it would always be a lie. I didn't ever want to trust anybody again, especially a male."

"I can't say that I blame you, but you have to stop running, and I plan on hiding those running shoes," he grumbled.

"You really don't see me as different?" I asked hesitantly. "You don't wonder if some of the genes I share with him could be bad?"

"Hell, no," he exploded. "Granted, I'd like to kill the bastard for the hell he put you through, and the innocent women who died, but you're beautiful inside and out, Brynn. I assume he's in prison?"

"He's dead," I said flatly. "Died in prison from cancer a few years ago."

"You didn't have any contact with him?"

"No. I couldn't. He was my nightmare. I had no desire to even see him as related to me. He destroyed mine and my mother's life. We were doing his life sentence with him because we had to deal with the guilt and shame that should have been his." I was still trembling, but I was slowly regaining my sanity.

"What happened with your mother that upset you so much tonight?" he said in a calmer tone.

"She did an interview with Marissa Waters. It's airing in a little under an hour. She said she needed to do it. She wants some kind of closure."

He nodded. "Maybe she's right. Maybe you need that, too. Not that I'm suggesting you do an interview. But it's obviously still raw for you."

"No way. I don't really want to talk about it. I talked myself to death over my years of counseling. I want to live my life in the moment. I just don't want to keep reliving the past."

"Maybe you need to close that door before you can move forward," he suggested huskily.

I thought about his words for a moment.

Had I ever really dealt with the truth, or was I just trying to sweep it under a rug? "I've never really had anybody I wanted to trust with my secret. The only one who knows is Laura, and she never pushed. I think she knew it was a sensitive subject for me."

"Then talk to me," he urged.

"I don't know what to say," I said softly. "It's like living with a stigma that will never go away. It's haunted every part of my life for fifteen years now, and I'm not sure I can let it go. I can't change my DNA. People are always going to judge if they know, and if I ever have kids, I'd have to explain what happened with my father to my children. How do you tell a kid who looks up to you that your father raped and killed so many women that we probably don't even know about them all?"

Carter lightly stroked my hair as he replied, "You can deal with that when you get there. Until then, you have to know that you're okay. Every family has their fair share of black sheep."

"I studied my family history. My father's family has been here in the United States for centuries. None of them ever had a history of violence. No murders. No black sheep. Not until him."

Checking out the family genetics had been an obsession for me. I hadn't been able to stop until I knew that there was nothing in my father's family history.

Carter's touch soothed me, and I let out a sigh.

"I don't know what to do to help you believe that none of this was your fault," he said, his voice tormented.

"Just being with me and knowing you're okay with this helps," I replied. "You have no idea how much it helps."

I'd felt so damn lost for so long that it was a relief to finally have somebody see *me* without seeing my father.

He wrapped his arms around my body and pulled me against him again, and I let myself relax.

I fell into the safety of Carter Lawson, and it was the most solace I'd ever experienced since the day we'd found out who my father really was, and what he'd done.

"I'll make you believe that just because you share some blood with somebody evil doesn't mean that you're anything other than perfect," he crooned next to my ear.

"I have to watch the interview. It's my mom. Will you watch it with me?" It would be so much easier if Carter was around.

"I'm not going anywhere," he said with so much conviction that I was starting to believe that nothing I could tell him would make him go.

I just hoped to God that I was right. I'd survived the guilt and shame of being a killer's daughter, but I probably wouldn't make it through seeing Carter Lawson leave.

Chapter 15

Carter

"I'm taking some time off," I told my two brothers on a video conference call the next morning from my home office.

I was going to get Brynn out of the city. She'd done okay watching the interview with her mom, but it had damn near torn my heart out.

I'd heard more about the trial because her mother had needed to testify, and about how people had shunned them after the news broke in their town.

Fucking judgmental assholes in their city had even sent letters and talked on the news about how Brynn and her mother could have prevented some of the deaths if they'd just paid attention.

For God's sake, Brynn had been a child, and people still got on their high horse, blaming her.

And the damage had torn Brynn and her mother both apart.

In many ways, I understood why Brynn's mom had needed to speak out. The lesson to her story was to blame the perpetrators and not the family. I'd gotten the message loud and clear.

Still, I wasn't sure Brynn had really understood. Not completely. She'd looked like she'd been torn up once the show was over.

"How much time?" Mason asked gruffly.

"I don't know. Maybe a few weeks. Could be a month." I had no idea how long it took to mend a heart, but I'd fucking keep at it until I fixed everything that had ever been done to Brynn.

"Where are you going?" Jett asked, sounding confused. "The engagement party is next month."

"I'll be there," I promised. "But something happened to Brynn. Something bad. I can't share it, but I need to help her. I need to get her out of the city for a while."

My plan was to escape to the mountain cabin I owned, and give her some peace.

"Is she okay?" Jett asked, sounding worried now.

"She's fine. It's not physical. But she needs me."

It felt good to say that the woman I cared about needed me, and I was kind of taken aback at how it made me feel like I was the only one who could help her right now.

"Take whatever time you need," Mason said firmly, like he was talking to an employee instead of his brother.

But it was kind of surprising that he hadn't missed a beat in giving me all the time I needed, even if it stretched out for a very long time.

"You need anything, man?" Jett asked sincerely.

"Maybe a manual on how to make a woman happy?" I said hopefully.

Jett chuckled while Mason grimaced. "Fresh out of those manuals," Jett answered. "If I finally figure that out, I'll let you know."

"Thanks for covering me. If it wasn't important, I wouldn't go," I told them.

"Carter, the company won't crumble if you're not here," Mason said.

"I know. But compared to you, I'll look like a slacker."

"You always have," he shot back.

An actual joke from Mason? I wasn't quite sure what to do with that.

"I'll be in touch," I answered.

"Call me if you need to talk or anything," Jett told me in a serious tone.

I nodded right before I cut the video chat session.

My mind wasn't on my company or my brothers at the moment. I was thinking about Brynn.

And the fact that if her evil parent wasn't already dead, I'd want to kill the bastard myself.

After everything she'd been through, all I wanted to do was protect her, make it impossible for her to ever be hurt again.

She was born to be a giving, brilliant, talented woman—which she was.

And she'd had to shine under a shadow for long enough.

How in the fuck can a man have a family, including a beautiful daughter of his own, and ruthlessly rape and kill young women along his truck route?

When they'd showed pictures of the victims during the interview, Brynn had completely lost it.

"We're getting the hell out of here," I mumbled to myself as I stood up, anxious to take Brynn somewhere that was peaceful and quiet.

I grabbed my bag and I was at Brynn's door within a few minutes.

Everything stopped when she smiled at me after she opened the door.

I was fucked.

And I knew it.

But I'd be damned if I cared.

"Hi," she said, still smiling as she waved me in.

"You ready?" I asked, anxious as hell to get her away from her own thoughts.

"Yes. But you still haven't told me exactly where we're going."

"I have a place in the mountains. Here. Take this."

She looked at me dumbfounded as I held out a card key that opened both the penthouse elevator and the door.

"I don't need a key to your place," she argued.

I picked up her bag that was already at the door as I said, "I want you to have it. If you ever need me, or if you ever need to see me, or you ever need to talk, just come up."

There was no way I ever wanted Brynn to need me and not be able to gain access to my door.

She looked hesitant, but I was relieved when she took it and put it in her purse. "You didn't have to do that, Carter."

"I wanted to," I said, my voice hoarse with the need to wrap her up inside me and never let her escape.

"Thank you," she answered, her tone more subdued than it had been.

"Let's go." I motioned toward the door.

Neither one of us spoke until we were in my black Lincoln Navigator and we were on our way to the mountains.

"I never pegged you as an SUV kind of guy," she mused.

"I only drive it when I'm going to the mountains."

"It's comfortable," she answered. "But it's big."

"Happen to have *a lot* of *big* things," I told her.

She laughed, just like I hoped she would. "Men who have to brag are generally overestimating."

"Not me. It's just a fact, baby," I joked.

"I'd call you out by asking to see for myself, but you're driving," she quipped.

"I could stop," I offered with way too much enthusiasm.

She giggled, something I'd never heard her do before. "Don't. We'd never get into the mountains."

My dick was instantly as hard as granite. I'd wanted Brynn for so damn long that I was pretty much getting used to having a constant erection. "We could stay in the city," I suggested.

Hell, I didn't give a damn *where* the first time happened for us. I just needed *something* to happen.

"The mountains sound like a romantic place for us to get naked for the first time," she pondered.

"This won't be easy for me, Brynn. You'll be way too close," I growled.

"Does this place of yours have a hot tub?" she asked innocently.

"Yes," I answered shortly.

"How fast can we get there?"

"It will take a while to get up there," I warned, now cursing the Seattle traffic that was going to slow me down.

Why in the hell had I decided to drive? I should have taken the helicopter.

"I can wait," she murmured. "Tell me about it? Is it a cabin?"

I nodded. "A *big* cabin."

"You never really do anything small, do you?"

I shrugged. "Generally not. And I bought it a couple of years ago. Haven't really been there much yet."

"Why?"

"I think I was pretty much just waiting for you," I answered, my voice coarser than I wanted it to be.

"You didn't even know I existed when you bought it," she said doubtfully.

"Maybe I just needed a reason to go. Going there sounded good in theory, but I never seemed to find enough time to get away. But it's nice there. Peaceful."

Honestly, I could hear my thoughts too loudly when I was there alone. I'd decided I needed to be around the constant hustle of work to drown them out.

"Thanks for this," she uttered in a genuine tone. "I think I need to get away."

"Everything will be okay, Brynn. You just need time."

"I've had time. I think I just need the right perspective. Maybe my mom was right. Maybe we do need to speak out about blaming the families. The way we were treated, and everything we had to go through to hide our identities, is crazy. I had to make excuses, or tell people that my father had died, even when he wasn't dead. I was a victim for a very long time. Maybe it is time to go on the offensive. At least for Mom. I can't speak out right now. I have a responsibility to my clients to keep the gossip about me at a minimum. But maybe someday I'll be ready."

"Until then, can you just be Brynn?" God, I hoped she could because she was special. She didn't need to be associated with anybody to shine.

"I guess that's something I'm willing to discover," she said wistfully.

"I think you're perfect just the way you are."

"You're an amazing man, Carter Lawson," she said with a sigh.

Hell, I could feel my ego swelling every time she stroked it, but I really needed her to pet something else, too. "I'm just a guy who wants you to be happy."

"I am," she answered immediately. "*You* make me happy. But I really want to make you happy, too."

"I'm a simple guy," I said. "Just get naked and I'll be ecstatic."

"Pervert," she accused.

"I never claimed that I wasn't warped." Hell, she made me so damn desperate that, for the first time in my life, I actually felt depraved.

"You know, I kind of like that about you," she said with a laugh.

"Yeah? What else do you like about me?"

"Hmm...you're pretty bossy, but nothing I can't handle. So it's attractive. And you're willing to eat anything I cook, which is good since I'm assuming I'll be cooking on this trip. You're pretty smart, and I'm discovering that I really like intelligent men."

"Not *men*," I demanded. "You like *me*."

As far as I was concerned, she didn't need to even discover if another guy was intelligent or not. I'd keep her so damn happy she wouldn't need to.

"I do," she said in a soothing voice.

"You sound tired. Are you?" I demanded to know.

"I didn't get a lot of sleep last night. I had a nightmare, and I haven't had one about my father in a long time."

I turned my head for a second, and saw the exhaustion on her face for the first time since I'd picked her up.

"You can sleep. I'll wake you up when we get there." There was no reason for her to stay awake.

"Then I'd miss talking to you," she answered in what she must have thought was a rational tone.

"We'll have plenty of time to talk while we're there." I hated the fact that she hadn't slept because she was scared. I wished I would have been there.

I was pretty damn determined to make every fear she'd ever had go away.

"Sleep. You will have to cook or we'll starve."

"Worried about your food source?" she said, giving me a hard time.

I'm worried about you!

"I don't like to see you exhausted," I admitted.

Not unless we've just had mind-blowing sex, and you definitely wouldn't look that weary.

She'd look utterly and completely satisfied.

"I think I'll live," I grumbled. "Go to sleep."

"I feel safe with you, Carter. I like that."

Hell, I liked that, too. But she had every reason to be scared. "You can trust me, sweetheart. I'd never do anything to hurt you."

Maybe I had been a prick. Maybe I still was, but not with her. Brynn had me by the balls. I just wasn't sure *she* knew that yet.

"I might fall asleep," she conceded.

I smirked. The only reason she was fighting it was because I'd insisted she sleep. But I wasn't complaining. Her stubbornness was one of the things that had gotten her through her early life. Brynn was a fighter, and I'd never want to see her any other way.

"I'll wake you up when we get there," I said quietly.

"I want that hot tub," she said, sounding like she was ready to give up the fight to stay awake.

"It will be ready for you," I promised.

I'd sent one of my assistants up by helicopter to make sure everything was ready when we got there, and that we were completely stocked with food.

I highly doubted that the hot tub would happen tonight since she looked like she was going to be out cold. But the sleep was better for her than getting in the hot tub tonight. Unfortunately, my imagination ran wild about finding her naked in that spa.

I hadn't been joking when I'd told her that it was going to be hard having her that close. It was going to be *very* hard the whole damn time we were in the same house. I'd be jacking off every damn night thinking about her. But I wasn't going to push until she was ready. She'd been through hell the last few days.

I heard a cute little snore from the passenger seat, and I grinned like an idiot.

She trusts me enough to keep her safe when she's vulnerable, when she's asleep.

I couldn't say why that made me happy. But my heart raced for a moment while I contemplated the fact that she really had passed out in my SUV without a second thought.

She fucking does trust me.

And that was way more important than my need to get her naked. At least it was for now. I'd worry about my painful erection later.

Right now, I had everything I needed.

Chapter 16

Brynn

I'*m definitely not going to need to work out today!*

I was actually short of breath by the time I reached the viewing area that had been mentioned with a small sign on the hiking trail.

But the view was definitely worth every bit of the pain it had taken to reach it.

It was wilderness for as far as the eyes could see, and the mountains were spectacular.

I took a deep breath and let it out slowly.

This was what I needed. I had to be reminded of how small I really was in the face of the vast space that was spread out before me.

Sometimes it was easy to forget how little my problems meant when considering the entire universe.

I wonder if Carter is awake?

I didn't remember much about the night before. I'd been so exhausted, but I did recall falling asleep on the drive up. After that... nothing. Somehow I'd woken up in Carter's bed early this morning with his arms tightly around me, and my head on his bare chest.

He felt so good that it had been hard to get up, and I didn't for at least a half hour. I'd just watched the sunrise, and basked in the feeling of being protected by a man who cared about *me*.

Obviously, he'd lugged me off to bed, and stripped off my clothes. I'd woken up in only my bra and panties.

I'd explored his "cabin" first, and it was big, just like he'd promised. It was all one level, but I'd counted five bedrooms and several bathrooms.

But it still had a country, homey feel to it. And it was decorated in a rustic style that I loved.

Once I'd gotten my bearings, I'd grabbed a pair of jeans and some hiking boots, went to a bathroom that wasn't close to the master so I didn't wake Carter, took a quick shower, and set out to explore.

From what I'd seen so far, I gathered we were in a popular hiking area. I'd seen occasional signs of previous visitors, but I hadn't run into anybody during my long walk.

I also hadn't seen any other homes.

The driveway of Carter's place was paved, but it looked like a dirt road to his house.

The sun was climbing higher in the sky, and I knew I should head back. I didn't have a watch or my cell phone, but I'd been gone for a while. Carter had satellite service set up for his house, but I was doubtful I would have gotten coverage out in the woods anyway.

I miss Carter.

Although the solitude had been therapeutic, I would have done anything to have him share this amazing view with me.

I shuddered as I thought about the pure temptation he'd been when I'd woken up with him. It wasn't like I didn't know that he was all muscle, and smooth, hot skin. But imagining it and experiencing it were two totally different things.

Somehow, our lives had become so entwined in such a short period of time that it was almost scary.

I turned and headed back down the steep incline, trying to watch my step. There were all kinds of hazards right beneath my feet.

"Brynn!" I heard the deep baritone calling out my name once I'd gotten close to the bottom of the steep incline.

Carter. He's definitely awake.

"Here," I yelled. "I'm coming down."

I could see Carter jogging down the hiking trail once I finally hit the path.

My heart flip-flopped, and I hurried to meet him.

"I'm sorry. I guess I lost track of time," I explained once he stopped in front of me.

"Goddammit, Brynn," he growled as he wrapped his arms around my body and squeezed me so tight that it was almost uncomfortable. "Where in the hell have you been?"

"Hiking," I squeaked. "I wanted to check the area out."

He finally pulled back, and his face was a mixture of fury and concern. "I woke up and you were gone. Your phone was still at the house. And there wasn't one damn sign of where you'd gone. I've been looking for hours. I almost didn't come this far."

"I didn't think I'd get phone service. I woke up at sunrise, and I wanted to explore a bit until you woke up."

"It's one o'clock in the afternoon," he said tersely.

"Oh, my God. I did lose track of time."

Carter might be angry, but he had a right to be. I probably would have freaked out if he'd done the same thing to me.

He grabbed my upper arms. "You scared the shit out of me, Brynn. I was ready to call the damn police."

"You were worried something happened to me," I said, slightly astonished by his turbulent expression.

The man looked terrified, and even though he was pretty magnificent in his ferociousness, I'd never want him to be this concerned. Not if I could help it.

"This isn't Seattle, Brynn." He shook me lightly. "There's a lot of nothingness out there. What if you got lost? What if you ran into a bear, or a damn mountain lion? You could die out here. So, hell yes, I was concerned."

I stared at his face, searching his eyes. He looked genuinely tormented, and it made me want to weep.

"I'm sorry, Carter. I didn't mean to be gone for so long. I'm used to going my own way, and not thinking about consulting with anybody else. Nobody else has ever worried about me," I said hesitantly.

"I fucking do, so you better get used to it," he said sharply as he took my hand and started back down the trail toward the cabin. "I give a shit about where you are, and if you're okay, especially in this environment, but I'm not even going to say that I wouldn't be worried if you took off like that somewhere else."

"Are you really mad?" I asked carefully.

He stopped and turned to me, his eyes still fierce. "Yes."

Jerking me close, he kissed me, his mouth descending like a ferocious summer storm.

This was a side of Carter I'd never seen, but I wasn't afraid of him. He was agitated because he'd been afraid something had happened to me, and all I wanted was to reassure him that I was more than fine.

I opened my mouth and let him consume me, and then pressed my body against his.

I got lost in the feel and the taste of Carter, and the passion that was raging between us.

There was nothing gentle or sweet about the embrace. It was pure desperation, and it wasn't just him who was feeling it.

I let myself feel every emotion that had been seething inside myself from the moment I'd met this man, and I let myself get lost in it.

Pressing my body closer, I could feel his rigid cock against my sex, and was frustrated as hell about the jeans and t-shirts that separated us.

I needed to feel him. I had to touch him.

Panting heavily as he released my mouth, I pleaded, "Fuck me, Carter. I need you."

"Goddammit, Brynn!" he said in a raw baritone. "I'm done pretending that I don't feel like this all the damn time."

I grabbed his hair and fisted it. "Then don't. Fuck me. Make the ache go away for both of us."

"If I do, there's no turning back," he warned me in an ominous voice.

"I don't care," I gasped, tearing at the t-shirt. "Let me touch you, Carter."

It didn't matter that we were in the middle of the woods. I had to satisfy both him and myself.

"Up there. Move it," he demanded, taking my hand again and lugging me up to rougher terrain instead of a well-worn hiking path.

The second we were beyond the view of the potential hikers, he pulled the t-shirt over his head, and I did the same thing, taking my bra along with it.

And then we were fused together again, my sensitive nipples abrading his bare chest as he kissed me as if our lives depended on it, which it actually felt like they did.

It was good. So good. And I tried to absorb Carter into me as I felt every inch of his bare skin that I could get to.

I moaned underneath the force of his mouth as his strong hand pushed between my thighs with hard, powerful strokes that rocked me, even though I was still wearing my jeans.

Carter was demanding that I give myself to him, which I did. Right now, he had me as vulnerable as a woman could get.

Our bodies fit together like they were made for each other.

He sunk his hands into my hair, tilting my head so he had the best access to my mouth, and kept tasting me like he was trying to get every morsel he could.

I nipped at his lips, egging him on, needing so much more.

I wanted everything he could give me, and then I needed it all over again.

My chest was heaving as I moved back to claw at the buttons of his jeans. "I need this. I need you," I pleaded.

He reached down and helped me unbutton his pants, and I finally gave up and worked on my own, startled that my hands were visibly shaking.

This is how much I want Carter. This is how powerfully he affects me.

I kicked off my hiking boots, frenzied to get naked.

Carter was already there the moment that I had my jeans and panties off.

He lifted me, and I wrapped my legs around his waist.

I released a whimper of relief at our bodies finally fused, both of us naked, our skin meeting with a profound sense of rightness that I couldn't explain.

It was bliss. It was hell. And I couldn't decide which one was stronger.

"Now," I demanded. "Right now."

He used a nearby tree to steady us, and cried out in pure elation when he surged inside me.

No mercy. And I didn't want any. I just wanted Carter so deep inside me that we didn't know where one of us ended and the other began.

"Yes," I said next to his ear. "Please."

I wasn't hesitant as I grabbed fistfuls of his hair and fused my mouth with his.

This was what I needed.

The moment was raw and beautiful, hard and tangible.

He pulled back, and then surged inside again. And again. Each stroke more forceful than the one before.

I reveled in the fast pace, and the way his fingers dug into my ass with our mouths still fused like we couldn't let go.

I ground against his cock every time he pummeled inside me, the knot in my stomach tightening.

When I surfaced to breathe, Carter growled, "Jesus! You're so damn wet and so tight, Brynn. So fucking hot, sweetheart. All I want is to make you come."

My body was in flames, but hearing his rough baritone infused with so damn much passion made my core clench around his cock.

I ground against him harder, putting pressure on my clit.

It felt so good that I kept doing it, over and over until I felt my climax rushing up to meet me.

And, sweet Jesus, did I come.

My orgasm rushed through me like a powerful tornado, and Carter gave me no quarter as he kept hammering into me.

"Carter!" His name was the only thing I could scream, my mind completely gone as my interior muscles clamped around his cock.

My fingernails dug into his back, and I heard him hiss, his body tightening as I milked him to his own heated release.

I panted as I slowly came back down to earth, and Carter let out the sexiest groan I'd ever heard as he loosened his grip on me. He still held me tight, but the viselike grip he had on my rear decreased in pressure.

"You nearly killed me," he snarled into my ear as he lowered my body to the ground.

It took us a moment to catch our breath, and Carter held me against him, cradling me, until we could finally breathe again.

My heart was still racing, but I eventually became aware of the world around us.

We dressed slowly, and it seemed like a shame when he started to cover the incredibly beautiful body that I'd just come against like I'd never climaxed in my entire life.

He helped me down the incline, and pulled me to his side when we hit the hiking path.

"Did we really just screw like that in the woods?" I teased gently.

He kissed the top of my head. "Yes, we did, Ms. Davis. You're a very naughty girl."

Euphoria was still zinging through my body as I answered. "Feel free to punish me any time, Mr. Lawson."

He whacked me playfully on the ass. "Be careful. I just might if you scare the hell out of me like that again."

Chapter 17

Carter

I felt like I'd waited forever to hear the sweet sound of Brynn screaming my name in ecstasy, and I'd done it with absolutely no finesse in the middle of the woods.

I wish I could say that I regretted it, but I'd be lying.

The moment I'd seen her completely unharmed after agonizing over where the hell she'd gone, I'd lost it.

It wasn't the way I'd planned it, or the way I'd fantasized about being with her. But fuck me, it was so much better than even my imagination could conjure up.

Luckily, she'd seemed just as happy as I'd been all day.

We'd ended up walking around for several hours, exploring a few of the things I'd seen when I'd been up at the cabin before.

And then we'd put some steaks and potatoes on the grill, and ate like we were both starving.

I started up the fire pit on the back patio, and slipped into the hot tub, knowing Brynn would be out shortly.

She was having a discussion with her mother on the phone, so I'd left her so she could have some privacy.

I appreciated the pressure of the jets and the warm water. I worked out, but I was pretty sure I'd used some muscles today that I hadn't in a very long time.

The jig is up. I can't hide the way I feel about Brynn anymore.

She made me crazier than I'd ever been, digging emotions out of me that I didn't know existed.

And she also made me happier than I knew I could be. Granted, I hadn't meant to be rough with her earlier, but that was just how she made me feel: out of control, and fucking terrified that if anything happened to her, I'd never survive it.

She pissed me off.

She amused the hell out of me.

She made me hard with just a smile.

And she made me completely lose my shit over something that she hadn't meant to do.

In short, I was fucked.

But I couldn't bring myself to give a damn about it.

"You're already in," Brynn said from the sliding door as she closed it behind her. "I don't even have my suit on yet."

I grinned at her. "Baby, I wish I was *in you*, and I'm not wearing a suit."

Our relationship had changed, and I loved the quick hint of a flush on her face as she got close to the hot tub.

"You're naked?"

I nodded. "As the day I was born. Who's going to see us? I don't have any neighbors. I own all of the acreage surrounding the cabin. The only thing that I don't own is the hiking paths, and they're not exactly close."

Brynn hadn't realized that she walked for miles earlier in the day, going across my property lines. Way farther than she should have.

She started to smile, her lips turning up with mischief, an action that had me standing at complete attention almost immediately.

She shrugged. "I have no problem getting naked then."

My damn heart nearly stopped as she tossed her gorgeous dark hair back, and her dark eyes met mine.

Brynn had an exotic, wild beauty that had drawn me in from the very beginning. And it wasn't only her external appearance.

Brynn could be lush and untamed, and she tempted me like no woman ever had before.

She was also intelligent, inquisitive, and probably the sweetest woman I'd ever known when she wasn't pissed off at me.

Her eyes had beckoned me, and something inside me had clicked into place, connecting me to her in a way that didn't make sense. Still didn't. But I was learning not to question something that felt as good as she did.

The protective, primal instincts to keep her close and protect her that I felt on day one had reared their ugly head today, and I knew they weren't going away. Nor were they going to be suppressed again.

I'd needed to be patient.

I'd needed to gain her trust.

She'd needed to be approached with caution, and I'd needed her to know that I wasn't going to go anywhere.

We'd gotten to know each other without sex. But damn, I was glad that was over with.

I adored every damn thing about her, but not giving in to the possessive instincts I couldn't control was just plain hell.

Mine. Brynn is fucking mine!

Funny thing was, I didn't even care that I was irrational when it came to her.

I was holding my damn breath as I watched her pull the t-shirt over her head.

I let it out when she paused.

"Don't tell me you're shy," I prodded her.

"I'm a model. It's my job to be sexy. I'm just letting you enjoy the show," she said in a provocative alto.

I watched as her jeans hit the concrete, and she kicked them to the side, her eyes running over me like she appreciated what she saw.

"Brynn," I said in a warning voice.

"Yes, Carter?" she said in an innocent tone that I knew was meant to provoke.

"Get in the hot tub."

Jesus Christ! I'd already fucked her like a guy possessed in the middle of the wilderness. I wanted to take my time the next time I got that naked body against mine.

"Just a minute," she answered as she ignored me and slowly released the front clip on her pretty, pink bra.

I had to stop myself from grabbing my aching dick and easing the pain myself.

Her breasts were so damn perfect that I gritted my teeth. They were more than a handful, and I nearly groaned as she touched one delicate pink nipple before she put two fingers under the elastic of her barely-there panties and lowered them slowly to her feet.

She kicked those aside and stood in all her glory, feet from where I was sitting in the hot tub.

Fuck! I didn't know if the water was suddenly boiling, or if it was me who was throwing off so much heat that I felt like I was going to burst into flames.

I knew I was staring at her pussy, but I couldn't help myself. She had a bikini wax, but wasn't totally bare. And that neat triangle was hot as hell.

Brynn obviously didn't have any kind of body issues. She didn't need to. But I could tell that her modeling career had made her pretty bold about posing in any state of dress—or in this case, undress.

Her confidence was seductive, but I knew I was going to have to suck it up about the fact that men lusted after my woman. I'd never ask her to give up her career until she was ready, but it was going to be far from easy to not let it bother me.

Thank fuck that her biggest contract was being the face of a cosmetics company, and I wouldn't allow myself to look at some of her previous shoots for bikinis or lingerie.

"You're right," she said as she stretched when she reached the steps to the tub. "Naked is definitely better."

"Get in the tub, Brynn," I said again, more desperate than I had earlier.

I wanted her in my bed.

I wanted to take my time.

There was no way I was screwing her in a hot tub.

Chapter 18

Brynn

I wasn't quite sure if the strip show had been for Carter, or if I'd done it for myself.

There was something titillating about having his gaze riveted on me like a hungry wolf eyeing probable prey.

He made no bones about the fact that he wanted me, and I hadn't had a guy I cared about look at me like that…ever.

Carter made me feel bolder than I actually was because I knew our attraction was mutual.

I sank down into the water, almost purring with the pleasure of the jets and the warm water. "I'm a little sore," I confessed.

"Probably because I manhandled you like a bull goes after a cow at mating season," he said wryly.

I flashed him a smile. "Maybe I like bulls," I teased. "I just haven't been with a guy for a while."

He reached out and snagged me around the waist, and then pulled me into him. "How long?"

"A couple of years," I admitted with a sigh. I'd gotten more stand-offish about having sex with a man just to have sex. My vibrator did the job just as well—sometimes better. "I'm pretty sure that I don't want to know how long it's been for you."

Carter was known for his prowess with women. I was pretty sure he hadn't been with someone else after we met, but I didn't want to hear about what had happened before that.

"Close to a year," he confessed as he toyed with my hair. "Regardless of what everybody thinks, I'm not indiscriminate when it comes to women, and I haven't met anybody I wanted to be with. I've been too busy trying to run everybody else's lives."

"So do you finally believe that you're not responsible for everything that happens in your world?" I asked softly.

"I don't want to admit it, but yeah, I think I do. I'm always going to want to control what I can, but I'm learning to let go of what I can't," he rumbled. "How about you? Are you feeling better?"

I nodded. "I had a long talk with my mother. I think she was right. She needed to tell her story, and I respect that. Now she's engaged."

"You say that like it's not a good thing," he ventured.

"It's not that. I guess I'm just afraid for her. But I haven't met her new fiancé, Mick. And she says he has his own future secure, and probably hers, too. But it's hard after what happened. I never want to see my mom destroyed like she was all those years ago." My disapproval had all been hinged on the fact that he could end up not being who my mom thought he was...breaking her heart a second time.

"Do you trust her to make a good decision?"

"I do. She had no way of knowing what my father was, and she's generally a pretty good judge of character. They've known each other for a while. Every relationship is a crap shoot, really."

"That's not exactly flattering," he said wryly.

"I didn't mean it like that, but how do you ever completely know somebody? We have to trust our instincts."

I felt him shrug. "Pretty much."

I leaned my head back on his shoulder. "Look at the stars. I haven't seen them this well since I was a kid. We lived in a fairly small town, away from the lights. I think I've forgotten how small a sky like this can make me feel."

There was only a sliver of the moon, but the stars were so bright that it kept the area from being completely dark. Along with the fire pit that Carter had lit, it was bright enough to see his face.

"Are you still planning your visit with your mom next week?"

"I am if you let me use your jet," I teased.

"It's yours whenever you need it."

"I have a long shoot at the end of next month," I told him. "Summer was slow, and I've been trying to slow down to work on the designing side, but my regulars are kicking back into gear. I'll probably be gone a lot until close to the holidays."

"Do you have a contract with anybody other than Easily Beautiful?"

"Nothing in writing, but I have companies that request me every year."

I wasn't sure why the idea of hitting the road again wasn't as exciting as it used to be. I suspected it was because I couldn't imagine not seeing Carter every day. But the constant travel had actually started to wear on me over the last year, too. Ever since I'd come to Seattle, I felt like I'd finally found my home.

"What about your bag designs? And the store?"

"I'm ready to do some prototypes," I told him excitedly. "And Laura has all the help she needs with the store. We switched our partnership agreement so she has full ownership. I'm just an investor. Her designs are brilliant."

"Any regrets?"

"None," I told him emphatically. "I get to be an early investor for a company that's going to explode, and I still get to work on my travel bag line. Laura never really needed me. She did an amazing job before I ever got here, and we're working together on social media."

"My brother Jett is having an engagement party in a couple weeks. I don't suppose you'd be interested in being my date?" he asked smoothly.

"I'd better be your date," I warned him. "As long as we're sleeping together, I'd really prefer if you didn't see anybody else."

Honestly, I couldn't imagine seeing him with another woman. It would destroy me.

"There is nobody else, Brynn," he said earnestly. "And there won't be. Hell, I spend too much time fantasizing about you."

I smiled. "Good. Keep it that way."

"You realize we didn't even discuss birth control," he contemplated.

Birth control had been the last thing on my mind earlier. I hadn't even been able to think once Carter had touched me. "I'm good," I informed him. "I had an IUD three years ago, so I have a couple of years. And I get tested regularly when I'm sexually active. Honestly, I don't let a guy touch me without a condom."

"I'm clean, too," he reassured me. "How did I get so lucky?"

"You drive me so insanely crazy that I didn't think about it," I admitted.

He tightened his arm around my waist. "You haven't seen crazy yet, sweetheart. But you will," he said in a husky voice.

I turned and straddled him. "I can't wait," I said a little too enthusiastically.

"I am not doing this in a hot tub," he said emphatically.

Really, the hot tub seemed like as good a place as any. All I knew was that I didn't want to let this man go for even a moment. It didn't matter what environment or what surface we were on.

I swiped a stray lock of wet hair from his forehead. "Then take me wherever you want me."

"That's the problem," he said gruffly. "I want you everywhere. It doesn't matter where we are or what we're doing."

I kissed him softly before I murmured, "I feel the same way. I always have. Even when you kissed me in the elevator, I wanted to tear your clothes off and force you to fuck me right there in the lift."

"There wouldn't have been any forcing, Brynn. I kissed you and I didn't even know you, an act I still don't fucking understand," he said unhappily. "I've never done that before."

I believed him.

There was some kind of crazy insta-lust that had sparked between us at first glance, and it was something I never would have said could happen.

"You and I are so similar in the most basic ways," I ventured. "Maybe you think that's crazy, but—"

"I don't think that at all," he interrupted. "We were both trying to outrun ourselves."

I nodded. "I recognized it in you because I see it in me. Both of us were so caught up in our guilt and fear about the past that we weren't really living the moments we were in. I tried. I really did. I wanted to be able to live in the present, but I couldn't get over my childhood trauma. Now, I don't really think it matters anymore."

He cupped my cheek as he rumbled, "I don't give a damn about the past, either. The only thing I want right now is you in my bed."

My heart stuttered. "Then take me there, Carter."

I squealed as he did just that.

Chapter 19

Brynn

My bare ass hit the bed as Carter dropped me there, and then came down on top of me.

"I want to take this slow, Brynn. I feel like we rushed to the finish line earlier, and never really experienced the race."

My breath caught as I saw the intensity in his eyes. "I'm not sure we know how to go slow," I said breathlessly.

"I'm sure as hell going to try," he promised as he lowered his head to kiss me.

That's all it took, the feel of Carter's lips on mine, and a rush of heat flowed between my thighs.

There was no brake for us. It was full-speed-ahead, can't-get-enough from that moment forward.

He was more deliberate, less out of control, but just as hot as he'd been in the afternoon.

I tried to wrap my arms around him to get closer, but he broke the embrace and pinned my arms gently to the side of my head before he said, "Easy, sweetheart."

I sighed as he kissed me one more time, and then started on the sensitive skin of my neck. "Carter, I'm not all that patient," I panted.

"I missed these earlier," he said against my heated skin as he palmed my breasts.

Even though I'd never been that much into long foreplay, the way Carter played my body made me close my eyes and feel every sensation.

The touch of his lips on my diamond-hard nipple.

His fingers plucking at the other one.

And my body tightened as he nipped at a hard peak, and then soothed it with his tongue.

My core constricted tightly, and then the flood of hot moisture that pooled between my thighs.

My back arched as the tormenting pleasure continued until Carter moved lower, his tongue tracing a line from my breast to lower abdomen.

"Please," I whimpered. "Carter, fuck me."

I speared my hands into his coarse hair, and held on. But as he moved between my legs, I let go and grabbed onto the bottom sheet, already anticipating what was about to happen.

I let out an animal-like sound as his hot tongue connected with my quivering flesh. "Oh, God, Carter. I can't handle this," I said desperately.

Pure pleasure coursed through my body as he took one long lick all the way up my pussy, and it felt so good that I was clenching the sheets like they were a lifeline.

He teased.

He tormented.

He lapped at my juices like they were some kind of sustenance he needed to survive.

And I shattered when he buried his face into my pussy and started to put everything he had into my pleasure.

I let out a long moan, my legs trembling.

Maybe I'd never been into foreplay because I had no idea it could be this damn good.

I squirmed beneath his mouth, my back coming off the bed as he put his fingers into the mix. He didn't stop putting pressure on my clit as those fingers fucked me, exploring every inch of my channel until he found a spot that nearly sent me to the roof.

"Yes. Yes. Yes," I chanted, completely lost in the sensuality of what he was doing to me. "Harder."

When his teeth clamped down on the tiny bundle of nerves begging for more attention, and then sucked, I imploded.

"Carter-oh-my-God-I'm-going-to-come," I screamed incoherently, my head thrashing on the pillow.

He thrust his fingers into me harder, faster, and the pressure on my clit sent me sailing over the edge.

I was still coming down from my orgasmic high when he rolled and pulled me on top of him.

"Ride me, Brynn," he commanded as he grabbed my hips, pulled them down, and seated himself deep inside me.

His cock was enormous, and felt like he was splitting me in two, but in a good way. I paused to adjust, to get used to his size and girth, before I raised up and sank back down on him.

It was a position I didn't have much experience with, but I loved the way I could see his face, his eyes, and the look of torment and pleasure in his expression.

Carter Lawson was beautiful, especially when he was this aroused. And I devoured him with my gaze.

"Tell me what you want," I said as I hesitated.

I wanted to make Carter feel the same intense heat that I did. I wanted to watch him lose himself in pleasure.

His fingers bit into my hips as he guided me. "Just this, Brynn. Just you."

I melted, recognizing that I made Carter vulnerable, as defenseless as I was right now.

He set a fast and furious pace, and I was just along for the ride. Every time I sank back down, completely taking Carter in, he consumed me.

It didn't take long before I could feel my orgasm building, and I welcomed it this time.

I wanted to splinter into tiny pieces because I knew that Carter would put me back together again.

"Fuck! Brynn!" Carter groaned as he slammed into me.

"Carter-I-think-I'm-dying," I screamed out as my climax rolled over me, the pleasure coming in waves that I rode along with the man I was watching as he found his own release.

I collapsed on top of him, and he held me tightly, our bodies covered in sweat.

Carter had just rocked my world, and I knew instinctively that nothing would ever be the same again.

Every emotion I had came rushing to the surface, and I had the ridiculous impulse to cry, even though I was blissfully happy.

"I take it you're still alive," Carter said hoarsely against my ear.

"Just barely," I retorted, unable to move a muscle, my breathing still slightly ragged. "I can't even move right now."

I knew my body would be screaming in the morning, but every moment of the pain I experienced would be worth it.

"I'd be happy to try to revive you," he said hopefully.

I could feel his cock already hardening beneath my sex. "Oh, no. I'm not doing that again tonight. You just wrecked me."

He chuckled as he stroked the hair out of my eyes.

I had no idea how Carter could have the desire or the fortitude so soon, but my body was completely spent.

"And I'm pretty sure we stink," I added.

"You smell like me and sex," he said, sounding completely content with the fragrance.

I rolled off him with a whimper.

"Are you hurt?"

I turned my head and smiled at him weakly. "Not in a bad way."

He jumped out of bed with more energy than I could muster, and then scooped me up as he said, "A warm shower should help."

I moaned with pleasure after he'd turned on the shower that had more jets than I could count, and pulled me inside.

"This feels amazing," I told him, my energy starting to come back.

The jets felt like they were pounding every sore muscle back to healthy tissue again.

Carter grabbed some soap, lathered up my body, and then rinsed me off before he reached for some shampoo.

Honestly, I'd never known how pleasurable it could be to have a guy wash my hair, but maybe it wasn't always that way. I was pretty sure it was the soothing way Carter massaged my scalp while he was getting my hair clean.

I felt like I'd gotten my second wind by the time my hair was completely washed and rinsed.

Grabbing the soap, I squirted a liberal amount into my hands before I dropped it back on the shelf. "My turn. I'm feeling very much revived."

I felt like I'd waited a lifetime to touch him like this, and there was no way I was going to waste the opportunity.

I caressed his chest, running my fingers over every muscle, and then I went for the six-pack abs. I couldn't resist putting my hand around his erect cock.

"Don't, Brynn," he cautioned.

"I just want to touch you," I said in a pleading tone.

"You might get more than you can handle," he answered in a disgruntled voice.

"I think I could deal with that," I muttered as I ran my fingers down his steely shaft. "Turn," I requested.

I soaped up his back, and then his rock-hard butt.

"I think you have the sexiest rear end I've ever seen," I commented.

"No, I don't," he shot back. "That honor definitely belongs to you, sweetheart."

He stepped in to rinse himself off.

"So you're an ass man?" I asked with a laugh.

"I'm totally into *any* part of your body," he replied in the completely wicked tone that I loved.

The man was charming, and I was pretty sure it came naturally to him.

We stepped out of the shower, and Carter dried my body carefully before toweling himself off.

"Do you want to come to Michigan with me?" My question came out far more awkward than it should have sounded.

He tossed the towel in the hamper and turned back to me. "I was already planning on it. I thought we could leave from here. Unless you really don't want me to go."

"I do. I just wasn't sure if you wanted to deal with the whole 'meet the mother' thing right now. We still don't know where this relationship is going to go. I thought you might want some time—"

"I don't," he interrupted in a firm tone. "Brynn, I want to meet your mother. She and your aunt are the only real family you have."

"She'll badger you about grandchildren," I warned him.

"Then I'll tell her that we aren't ready for that."

"She's opinionated and blunt," I added.

He grinned. "Then I guess I know where you got those traits."

"Smartass," I said, my heart light.

I wanted Carter to go with me, but I'd been afraid it was way too soon for him to get wrapped up in family.

"If you think I'm bad, wait until you meet my brothers," he said in a falsely beleaguered voice. "And you're meeting my family shortly, and there is a hell of a lot more of them than I have to meet in Michigan."

"I can't wait to meet them," I told him sincerely.

It boggled my mind that there were more Lawson brothers, two sisters, and Harper's kids.

And every one of his siblings was successful at whatever they'd chosen to do in life.

His parents must have had incredible genes.

"Bedtime," he said roughly as he grasped my hand and pulled me back to the bed.

"We've already been there once."

He pulled me down with him onto the rumpled sheets as he said, "We're sleeping this time."

We got comfortable, and I straightened out the top sheet as I said, "You sure about that?"

He reached over me and shut off the light. "Positive. No matter how much I'd love to hear you screaming my name when you come, I want you to be able to walk tomorrow more."

My mind was screaming in protest, but I knew he was right. I wanted to enjoy every intimate moment that Carter and I had together.

He was planning to take me into the nearest town tomorrow, and it would suck if I wasn't able to explore with him.

He wrapped his arm around me and pulled me against his side.

I put my head on his chest with a sigh.

He put my needs before his own, and that was when I knew I was totally, completely, and head-over-heels in love with Carter Lawson.

That should probably terrify me, but it didn't. Maybe I'd gotten used to trusting someone, and my fears didn't haunt me anymore. Or maybe I'd...changed. Having Carter accept me for all that I was had lifted the black cloud over my head, and he'd helped to convince me that I really was okay, murderous father and all.

"Thank you," I murmured against his bare shoulder.

"For what?" He sounded puzzled.

"For this trip. For putting my needs before yours. For worrying about me. For caring if I'm happy. And for accepting me, no matter what. Should I go on?"

"You don't have to thank me for caring about you, Brynn," he answered.

"Maybe I don't, but I wanted you to know how much it means to me. And I want you to know that I feel the same way about you."

He kissed me, his embrace filled with promise, but gentle at the same time.

Moments later, I was asleep.

Chapter 20

Brynn

"How's the visit with your mom going?" Laura asked while we were in the middle of a video chat.

We'd spent about thirty minutes discussing her clothing line and the designs for my handbags.

We were only just getting to the personal stuff.

Carter and I had stayed in the mountains for almost a week, having sex in almost every room of the "cabin," and now we were in Michigan visiting with Mom.

"Fine. But she's already asked every embarrassing question I could think of, and more."

Carter had managed to get into my mother's good graces already, so I wasn't worried about the two of them being together at the mall.

I'd stayed behind so I could chat with Laura.

"He's your boyfriend now, right? You know she's going to grill him," Laura said with a teasing expression. "Does she like him?"

"Too much," I answered with a sigh.

Honestly, it had been a relief that Carter had been able to charm my mother, but I knew, in her head, Mom was already planning her grandkids and wondering what they'd look like.

Aunt Marlene, who had ridden along with them, seemed to adore Carter just as much.

"And I'm not sure he's really my boyfriend," I added.

"You're sleeping together," she countered.

I hadn't needed to share that fact. Since I'd been shacked up in a mountain cabin with Carter, she'd made her own assumptions.

I nodded. "But you and I both know that sleeping together doesn't make a lover a boyfriend."

Her eyes widened. "Come on, Brynn. This is *me* you're talking to. You've never been this way with any other guy. I can tell you're crazy about him. And I know he feels the same way about you. I think he realized it before you did. I could tell when we ran into each other at your condo."

I shrugged. "We haven't really talked about a future together, Laura. We both have busy lives."

"You will when you're ready. Does he know about your father?" she said in a softer voice.

"Yes. And he's been amazing about it. It doesn't matter to him, Laura."

She crossed her eyes. "Duh. Of course it doesn't. It had nothing to do with you."

"I think I'm actually starting to believe that," I confessed.

"It's okay to take it slow if you want to," she suggested. "But don't think he won't be wanting a future."

"I'm in love with him," I blurted out to the only person I'd trust with that information.

She smiled. "I know. I can tell. Everything will be okay, Brynn. I know you're always waiting for the other shoe to drop, or for something to go wrong, but it won't this time. I can feel it."

I grinned back at her. "I don't know what happened. We really couldn't be more different."

"Only on the surface," she stated. "And really, it isn't that unusual for a model with your popularity to be married to a man who's loaded."

"The funny thing is, our money was never even an issue," I said wistfully. "I love Carter for the man he is, not the billionaire."

I heard voices coming into the house.

"They're back," I warned Laura.

"I'll let you go," she offered.

"You better say hello to Mom. She's been talking about how long it's been since she's seen you."

Laura had often come home with me for the holidays. So she knew and liked my mother a lot.

"Are you still talking to Laura?" my parent asked as she came through the front door.

I was sitting on the couch, so I turned the screen in Mom's direction.

"Oh, hi honey," my mother said excitedly as she waved at Laura and moved closer. "I saw your swimsuit layout in that women's magazine last year. You looked beautiful."

Mom chatted away with Laura while my eyes automatically looked behind my parent for the man who always drew my attention.

He moved to my mother's side and bent down to kiss me sweetly. "I missed you," he whispered huskily in my ear after he released my lips.

My heart skipped a beat. I'd missed him, too.

"Laura, this is Carter. Have you met him?" my mother asked as she drew my man right next to her.

"I have. Nice to video see you again, Carter," Laura said in a chirpy, polite voice.

"The pleasure is all mine, Laura," he said smoothly. "How's the business going?"

"Really good," she told him. "Thanks for meeting with my marketing manager to help her make a plan."

Carter was already doing as much as he could to get a marketing plan going for Laura's clothing line. He was also trying to talk her into letting him become an investor since he wanted to ramp up bigger than either one of us could afford.

"My brother, Jett, is having an engagement party in a couple of weeks. Would you like to join us?" he asked Laura.

"I'd love to," she answered. "Just have Brynn send me the details."

I finally turned the screen back in my direction, and Laura and I ended the session after agreeing to get together as soon as I got home.

I closed the laptop as Carter sat down beside me on the couch, and my mom went to put her purchases away.

"Why did you ask Laura to Jett's engagement party?" I asked curiously. "I thought it was mostly family."

"Family and a bunch of other guests," he said with a smirk. "The guest list keeps getting longer. If he doesn't stop asking people, he's going to run out of room in his penthouse."

"Maybe he'll be mad that you asked somebody he doesn't know," I said.

"Never," he replied. "And Laura is pretty much your family. But that isn't the only reason I wanted her to come. I like her, and I think my older brother does, too."

"Mason?" I said with surprise. "He doesn't know her."

"He saw her at that charity benefit," he informed me with a smirk. "It's the first time I've seen Mason interested in anything other than business, much less a woman. I'm starting to think that he never gets laid."

I crossed my arms and tried to give him an admonishing look. "Are you playing matchmaker?"

"Not my usual style, but yeah, this time I am."

I laughed. "Then I'll tell you that Laura thought he was hot, too. But I'm not sure Mason is her type."

There was a mischievous look on his face as he answered, "She's *his* type."

"But you said he's only obsessed with Lawson Technologies."

He shot me a heated look. "I think we both know that when the right person comes along, we can easily be distracted from work. Mason is a good man. He was actually the kindest of all my siblings when we were kids, going out of his way to help anybody who needed it. I know that guy is still in there somewhere."

I swallowed hard because Carter's voice revealed a little bit of longing to find the older brother who had somehow gotten lost and caught up in his business to the point where Mason didn't think about anything else.

"We're already assuming that sparks will fly," I told him.

"I know they will," he said confidently.

"Then I'm glad you invited her."

I wasn't about to reveal that Laura was starting to look at getting a baby daddy from a test tube. It was too personal. But my best friend deserved everything.

The loving husband.

Her flourishing business.

And the child she so desperately wanted.

It wasn't that I wasn't supportive of her going it on her own. She was perfectly capable of raising a child by herself, but for her, I wanted...more.

I grabbed Carter's polo shirt and pulled him toward me. "You're a good man, Carter Lawson."

What billionaire would ever try to play matchmaker just on the possibility that it might make his older brother happy?

He wrapped his arms around me. "So you keep saying," he answered hoarsely, his breath warm on my lips.

"Believe it," I murmured as I pulled his mouth to mine.

Carter wasn't perfect, but he was everything I'd always wanted. I just hadn't realized it immediately.

He made me happier than I'd ever dreamed possible.

So why was there a little sliver of my soul that was terrified about that?

Chapter 21

Brynn

"I'm getting completely and totally spoiled," I said to Carter as his private jet lifted off to take us back to Seattle. "It's nice to travel like this."

I loved my parent, and spending time with her and my Aunt Marlene, but I was anxious to have Carter to myself again.

Not knowing exactly what our relationship was when we'd arrived, Mom had put us in separate bedrooms, and I'd been so self-conscious about the idea of her knowing that I actually had sex that Carter and I had just suffered through it.

"Guess it's a damn good thing you have the man who owns the jet," he said in a husky tone. "I'd really prefer that you travel this way. It's a lot safer than having layovers everywhere."

What was he saying? "Carter, I'm not going to take your jet whenever I need to get somewhere."

"Yes, you are," he countered highhandedly. "I just haven't convinced you to do it yet."

I smiled. "You do realize that I've traveled all over the planet alone for over a decade, and nothing has happened to me yet."

I'd become very good at traveling, getting myself organized so much that the trips went as smoothly as possible.

"You've been lucky," he grunted. "But you've been victimized by thieves."

"Which is bound to happen to somebody who travels as much as I do." When I was building my career, I took every single job I could get, and I was on the road more than I was home throughout those years.

"Not anymore," he said firmly.

I opened my mouth to say something, but when he entwined our fingers together on the armrest, I shut it again.

Traveling safer was something we could talk about when we actually decided what we were to each other, and if this was going to be long-term.

It wasn't exactly a compromise to travel in a private jet.

I sighed and leaned my head back against the cushiony, butter-soft headrest of my seat.

"I actually liked Mick," I confessed. "Did you?"

"I did. He seems like a pretty good guy, and his background check was squeaky clean."

I turned my head, flabbergasted. "You actually checked him out?"

"Of course. You weren't going to relax until you knew that he didn't have any nefarious intentions. But I told him that I did it."

My jaw dropped. "What did he say?"

"Actually, he was pretty cool about it. He understands that this is difficult for you, and he has enough balls to roll with it. The guy has nothing to hide, Brynn. He's owned his own businesses since he was young, and he's been successful. He's more than financially secure, and I think he really does love your mother."

"What else?" I asked breathlessly.

Maybe it had been presumptive of Carter to check out Mick's background, but I had to admit that any doubts I'd had about him marrying my mom were fading away.

"He's donated a lot of money to charity over the years, he's built homes for the disadvantaged with no financial gain, and he can give your mom a great life. Not that you haven't done that already," he drawled.

"Thank God," I said on a sigh of relief. "He seemed really nice, and he seemed like he loved Mom, but sometimes—"

"It's over, Brynn," he interrupted. "The past is behind you and it's definitely put to rest for your mother. Mick isn't going to hurt her. He wants to retire and travel with her. He just wants to make her happy."

I hadn't realized how many doubts I still harbored, even though Mick had been a very nice man. "I'm glad he wasn't angry. I'm not sure how I'd feel if somebody had to check out my background to like me."

"The guy had nothing to hide. So he didn't care. I think he just wants you to be okay with their relationship."

"I am," I said in a tremulous voice. "I was just afraid. It had nothing to do with him exactly."

"He knows that," Carter said in a soothing voice. "And he understood that you weren't going to let go until you knew everything about him."

"How do you always know what I need before I do?" Not in a million years would I have considered doing a background check on my mother's fiancé. But now that Carter had, I was relieved.

"Maybe because my primary purpose in life right now is to make you happy," he said lightly.

I searched his eyes, and I could see nothing but truth, even though his voice was slightly teasing. "You do," I said in a whisper because it was hard to get the words out.

And I wanted to make him happy, too. There was nothing I loved more than seeing Carter ecstatic.

I unbuckled my seat belt now that we were at cruising altitude, and stood. I unbuckled his restraint, making sure I brushed over his cock several times in the process.

"Come to the bedroom with me?" I entreated.

Carter was up so fast his muscular body was almost a blur. He took the lead and tugged me along behind him until we were in the bedroom at the back of the jet.

The door closed loudly behind us as he pushed it closed.

"Jesus, Brynn! I've missed you in my bed so damn much," he growled as he took me roughly into his arms and kissed me.

We exchanged a passionate kiss like we'd been apart for years and not just a week.

I ached for him, but I wasn't going to surrender right now. I wanted to see Carter lose it, and I wasn't going to be happy until I did.

When we surfaced, I told him adamantly, "This time, I'm in control."

He gave me a hungry look, but he didn't argue.

I pulled the polo shirt over his head, and tossed it aside. And then started on his jeans.

"So you're just planning on having your way with me?" he said in a teasing but rough tone.

"Yep. That's the plan. You got a problem with that?" I questioned.

He slowly shook his head. "I'm all yours, sweetheart."

My heart tripped. I wanted Carter to be mine. I was still in awe of the fact that this powerful, strong, gorgeous man was with me, and cared about me.

And to have unfettered access to him was heady as hell.

I dropped down to my knees and took his boxers and jeans to the floor. He kicked them off, and we landed with a tumble on the king-sized bed.

Keeping Carter on his back, I said, "Don't move."

"Do you really think I'd want to be anywhere but exactly where I am right now?" he asked gruffly.

Carter was an alpha male, and he liked to be in control. But for once, I wanted to test his limits.

I stared down at all his hot, naked, totally masculine body, and I melted. "You're the hottest man I've ever seen," I breathed out in awe as I put my lips on his chest.

I'd wanted the chance to explore Carter the way he did to me, but things had always gotten too hot and heavy for me to have that opportunity.

I took it happily now as I nuzzled, licked, and kissed my way over every hard muscle on his chest, and traced his six-pack abs with my tongue.

I could feel his body tensed when I was done. "Relax," I crooned.

"I can't," he shot back. "You're killing me, Brynn."

I wrapped my hand around his rock-hard cock. "Maybe this will help."

I got lost in touching the silken skin over his shaft, and stroking the moisture onto my finger at the tip of the velvety head.

He watched intently as I closed my eyes and sucked his essence from the tip of my finger.

I opened my eyes then, and stared back at him as I said, "I want more."

"Fuck! Brynn. I can't," he exploded.

"Don't stop me this time," I insisted as I moved so I could taste him.

Carter had always kept me from getting him off. I knew it was because he didn't want me to go unsatisfied. What he didn't understand was that I would be completely gratified if he'd just let me make him come.

The first taste was heaven as I took as much of his shaft as I could, moaning at the taste of him.

He groaned something incoherent, and I went to work in earnest to bring him as much pleasure as possible.

Every tormented groan he released flooded my pussy with moisture, but it was music to my ears as I increased the suction, going down on him over and over again.

"Enough!" he demanded.

I surfaced long enough to say, "Not happening, big guy."

I squealed as he sat up enough to lift my body, turn it, and pull my core over his mouth.

I shivered as I felt his hot breath hitting my quivering, slick flesh. I moaned as he grabbed my ass and pulled my sex onto his face.

The pleasure was so intense, Carter's mouth so hungry that I lowered my head and gave him the same voracious ecstasy as he was giving me.

The position was unfamiliar, but I was so lost in sensation that it didn't matter.

Everything in my belly unfurled as my orgasm hit me, my body quaking as Carter finally, finally gave me the chance to really taste what it was like to make him come.

I swallowed every drop, my body trembling as my tongue tried to lick him clean.

But he lifted my body before I could finish, and pulled me up next to him. He immediately swooped down to kiss me, and I felt like I was almost drowning in the taste of us mingled together as he kept up the passionate embrace.

I was still panting when he released my lips, and I buried my face in his neck.

My body hummed as I caught my breath.

Carter was nuzzling my face as he said, "You can have your way with me anytime you want."

My heart was so light that I laughed, and then nipped at his neck playfully.

God, I loved this man so much that my heart felt like it was ready to explode.

My entire being felt alive, and before Carter, I wasn't sure I'd ever felt that way.

I'd existed.

I'd made myself as happy as possible.

I'd been content.

But he'd awakened a part of me that I hadn't even known existed.

And I knew I never wanted that part of myself to go dormant ever again.

Chapter 22

Brynn

"Thank you for letting me take a look at these. I saw the hype on social media, and I knew we needed to meet."

I looked at the older female sitting across from me and blinked. Never in my wildest dreams had I imagined that my prototype purses would cause this big of a stir.

When Carter and I had come back from visiting my mother, I'd made it a point to get the bags I'd designed mocked up so I could test them for travel while I was gone on assignment.

I hadn't expected the biggest name in designer bags to offer to buy them.

We'd ended up meeting at a café close to my condo. She'd come to my location just to talk to me.

"I'm not sure I want to sell, Ms. Waverly," I said truthfully. "This line means a lot to me. I want to make sure that style and function stay in all of the purses."

"Of course," she said with a nod. "And please call me Alicia."

"They're just mock-ups right now, Alicia."

"I want this line, Brynn. When I saw them, I understood why everybody wants one. I travel, too," she said with a small smile. "I've had the same frustrations, and we could find a way to make sure the line has your name, and your approval before every new one is produced."

If I'd ever wanted to do a new line of purses, this company was the one I'd want behind me.

They were a very popular luxury brand, but not so expensive that they would limit the market of women who wanted to buy one.

"I'd like to think about it," I said earnestly. "If I wanted a partner, your company would be it. It's a great line without pricing a lot of women out of the market. I've always appreciated that."

"I'll write up the contract…just in case," she said with a determined expression. "If you decide to go with us, which I know you will, we can start the negotiations."

She was tenacious. I'd give her that. But women's fashion was a tough field. At least she was aggressive without being completely obnoxious.

"Thanks for coming," I said as I put the purses back into the carry bag I'd brought them in. "I'll get back with you soon."

She stood and brushed imaginary wrinkles from her professional skirt and stylish jacket. "If you wait too long, I'll be calling you. By the way, I know a company who'd really love to talk to Laura about her clothing line, too."

I smiled as I rose. "I doubt very much if she's going to be interested. She's definitely going that line on her own. I'm an investor, and she has interest from some pretty deep pockets to be investors, too."

"Well, if she changes her mind, send her to me."

Laura had already had offers, and I knew she wasn't interested in launching within a company. "Definitely," I said, just to keep from being rude.

We went our separate ways outside the café, and I decided to walk since I was within a mile or so of my condo.

I can't wait to tell Carter what happened.

It was funny that he was always the first person I thought about, whether my news was good…or not so good.

Our lives had become so entangled that I could hardly have a thought without wanting to share it with him.

I quickened my step just a little because Jett's engagement bash was tonight, and I wanted plenty of time to relax and get myself ready.

Most of the time, when we were home, Carter was with me in my condo. We spent almost every night together, too.

I was weaving my way around all the people hurrying down the sidewalk when a dark head inside a store caught my eye.

Carter?

I stopped right in the middle of the sidewalk, and I heard a few disgruntled mumblings as people moved to avoid me.

What was he doing here?

It was a fine jewelry store, one of the most exclusive in the city.

His back was to me, and my heart dropped as he turned his head, giving me a profile of him. I noticed that he was talking to a woman beside him.

No! He's not with her. He just met her in the store, I'm sure.

I checked them out, watching, even though I knew I probably shouldn't.

Carter had told me that he had a meeting this afternoon, so I wouldn't see him until he picked me up for Jett's party.

I'd almost convinced myself that it was innocent until I saw him put his arm around the female and then kiss her on top of the head the way he always did to me.

My heart squeezed in my chest so hard that it was physically painful, and I forced myself to move forward.

There really was no excuse anymore. He was cuddling up to the woman, giving her the same affectionate pecks to the top of her head that he did to me.

Relax. Maybe there's still an explanation.

Although I couldn't imagine why he'd be in a jewelry store, apparently picking out something for the woman he was with.

It made me nauseous that I'd seen several of those jewelry boxes myself, gifts that Carter seemed to give frequently.

A beautiful ruby bracelet.

Then a matching necklace.

And I'd gotten the earrings to go with the set only a few days ago.

I pulled out my phone, and clicked on Laura's number.

I wasn't sure how she understood my rambling explanation, but she apparently got the gist of it.

"Brynn. Don't jump to conclusions. I know it's easy to do under the circumstances, but there could be an explanation. I don't believe that he'd be with another woman," she said emphatically.

"Things aren't always as they seem," I said tearfully.

I knew that kind of disappointment, and the disbelief that happened when somebody turned out to be a completely different person than the one you knew.

"Don't torture yourself like this, Brynn. Talk to him first. Yes, it's possible that he's really a dog, but I don't think he is. He doesn't seem to see any other woman except you," Laura told me. "Make sure it isn't a mistake."

"I won't see him until he picks me up for Jett's engagement party."

"Then talk to him after it's over. It's not like you're going to part. You live in the same building."

I wiped a stray tear from my cheek, pissed off at myself because I was crying. "I should have known better than to make a man my entire life, Laura. I never wanted to be that woman who falls apart when it's over."

"It is not over," she said firmly.

Carter would have to have a damn good explanation for it *not* to be over.

And I couldn't think of a single one right at the moment.

Not when he'd been holding her the way he did me.

Not when he'd kissed her with apparent affection.

"I'll talk to him," I said. "But I don't know what he can say to make what I saw make sense."

"If he's cheating on you, I'll cut his balls off for you," she answered. "But give him a chance to tell you what happened first. I'd usually be the first one to tell you to run away, but not with Carter. I can tell that he cares about you."

"Sometimes caring isn't enough," I replied, knowing that if Carter had his eyes on another woman, I could never give him a second chance. "I have to know I can trust him. He's always going to have women clamoring to be with him."

"And you don't have guys who would give anything to be with you?" she asked.

"I don't care about them," I said tremulously. "I don't sleep with them. They don't mean anything to me."

"So what does it matter how much other people want to be with either of you?"

Problem was, I didn't know if Carter felt the same way, and from the looks of things, he didn't take this relationship nearly as seriously as I did.

After promising Laura that I'd hold my verdict until Carter had a chance to plead his case, we hung up.

I entered my building, but before I could get to the elevator, the receptionist waved at me.

"I have a delivery for you, Ms. Davis," she said in a far too cheerful voice. "Flowers."

The arrangement was beautiful, and I took the heavy vase from her hands, and held it with my free arm. I gave her a smile before I turned away, but I wasn't able to speak.

I took the elevator, and I was in my condo before I opened the card. Not that I really had any doubt who the flowers were from.

Every moment that we aren't together is mediocre. Every moment that you're with me is memorable. I can't wait to see you tonight. C.

My heart didn't skip a beat like it usually did.

And I wasn't breathless with excitement.

I didn't feel much of anything as I gathered up the purses I'd showed Alicia and went into the bathroom to take a bath.

Unfortunately, even the hot water I submerged myself in couldn't take away the chill of knowing I was going to lose Carter.

I wasn't sure I'd ever be warm again.

Chapter 23

Brynn

"I heard that you're going to Hollywood, Brynn. What's it like there?"

I smiled at Ruby, Jett's fiancée, while the party was in full swing around us. "It's just a commercial. And Los Angeles will be nice now that it's cooling down in California. I don't know how to explain Hollywood exactly, but you might be disappointed. It's not all that glamorous if you look around too much. You'll find homeless people everywhere, and it seems weird with all the wealth in the area. It's kind of...sad."

I'd adored Ruby almost from the moment I'd met her. She was young, only twenty-three, but I could sense an old soul.

We'd snuck off to a small table in the corner of Jett's impressive penthouse so we could talk, and I'd been grateful to get out of the middle of the festivities. I'd tried to act like nothing had happened, but I felt completely destroyed.

I was good at hiding my emotions, but I could only do it for so long.

Carter had picked me up in a tuxedo, and I had on my favorite little black dress, but nothing felt the same.

"I was homeless once," she informed me. "For a very long time. Jett is helping me work on improving the lives of the homeless here in Seattle."

I knew Ruby had experienced a lot of trauma, but the fact that she'd been homeless surprised me. "I have to admit that I was close to that state myself in my early years. But you're so young, Ruby."

"I was a teenage runaway. I had no place to go. But then I met Jett. I didn't trust anybody until I met him." She was candid and brutally honest. I respected that.

"I've had my share of trust issues," I shared with her before I took a long sip of my champagne.

There was something about this woman that I connected with. Maybe it was the fact that we'd both been cheated out of our childhood and teenage years. Honestly, I couldn't imagine what it would have been like to be so young and on my own. If nothing else, I'd always had my mother.

"How did you meet?" I asked, curious now.

"He rescued me," she said with a wistful sigh. "I was being held captive by human traffickers. I'm not sure where I would have been if it hadn't been for him. I've built my own business now, so I'll always know that I can take care of myself, but I couldn't imagine being anywhere without him. He's my best friend."

Talking to Ruby made me realize just how sheltered I'd been in some ways. Sure, I'd been hungry during those slim years in New York, and there were months I wasn't sure I could pay my rent. But I'd never been through what Ruby had. "I'm not sure I would have survived."

She shrugged. "It's strange what we do when we're forced to survive. I think you can handle a lot more than you think you can. You've just never been in a position where you had to fight to live."

I shook my head. "I haven't."

"I learned as I went along. Moved to a warmer climate because it was cold outside, found places where I could find food, and stayed out of trouble. Well, for the most part anyway. The traffickers were unexpected, but I was desperate to find a job. Any job."

"And they made you think you'd get one?"

She nodded.

"Bastards," I said angrily. "I hate men who prey on vulnerable women."

Obviously, it was a personal thing because it was exactly what my father had done.

Ruby smiled. "Me, too. I'm working on changing as much as I can in my little part of the world."

"I'd like to be involved. Can I?" I questioned.

"We're working on putting together a foundation," she informed me. "I'm sure we'll still be in touch since you're Carter's girlfriend."

I had to stop myself from visibly flinching. "I'd be willing to do whatever would help. Even if it means making beds in shelters or whatever manual labor you need," I told her. "I'm a decent cook."

"Aren't you already involved in a lot of charities?" she asked. "Carter said he met you at a domestic abuse fundraiser."

"I am. But that's just a check. I've never had the time to be personally involved because I travel so much. And Carter and I didn't exactly meet that night. We just saw each other." I really wanted to get away from the subject of her soon-to-be brother-in-law.

"I know. You gave him a gigantic slap-down," she said with a laugh. "And I'm sure he deserved it."

"He told you that?" I was definitely surprised that Carter shared the fact that I'd given him the cold shoulder.

"He was feeling pretty bad, Brynn. I'm glad you gave him another chance. Carter seems superficial and cold on the surface, but he's really not like that."

"What do you think he's like?" I really wanted to get Ruby's perspective on him.

"Lonely until he met you. And I think he feels responsible for every problem anybody who's close to him has. I can't believe he actually blamed himself for his parents' deaths just because they went out of the house to get him something. But that's just how

Carter is. He doesn't wear his emotions on his sleeve, but he feels things pretty deeply."

Suddenly, I wanted to cry. She'd just put Carter's personality into a nutshell. Maybe there was a lot more than she ever saw, but she was pretty spot-on. "He told you about his parents?" He hadn't shared that with me.

"After he told you, he talked to Jett. And then he shared his feelings with all his siblings. Every one of them told him it was crazy for him to feel that way. I think he's feeling a lot better since he talked to his family." Ruby drained her champagne glass and motioned for another.

I swiped one myself, even though I'd probably already had as much as I should have for the evening.

"I'm so glad he met you, Brynn," Ruby said after she took a small sip of her full glass. "He seems so happy." She nodded toward the siblings, who were all talking and laughing in the middle of the room.

I watched Carter, his expression animated as he spoke to his sisters and brothers, and he did look happy.

It was kind of like déjà vu. I'd seen him like this across the room at a party, looking elegant and sophisticated in a tux, and back then I'd seen him as a fraud, just like me.

Now, he was still pretty damn comfortable in his own skin, but his eyes were far from cold. And he was genuinely enjoying his family.

"If I'm not with Carter, will you still stay in touch?" I asked.

Obviously the champagne was getting to me. I was feeling melancholy, and I was rarely that gloomy.

"Of course," she said immediately. "But you'll still be with Carter, won't you? I mean, you two are perfect for each other, and I know he adores you."

I gave her a weak smile. "I hope I will be. We haven't really gotten it all figured out."

"We'll exchange numbers before you go," Ruby insisted. "But I don't think you're going anywhere, except maybe to Hollywood. Do you have other traveling to do?"

"I'm on the road a lot," I shared. "But I just got an offer from an enormous brand to produce my line of travel bags with them. If that gets off the ground, I probably won't be globetrotting as much."

"That's fantastic, Brynn. Is it the bags you've been showing on social media? I follow you, and they're amazing. I want one, but Jett says they haven't been released yet."

"I'll send you some if I start getting them produced. What you saw were just the mock-ups."

Her eyes left my face, and I could see her glancing at her fiancé occasionally. The love she had for him was evident.

Maybe on the surface, the beautiful woman in the startling red dress across from me seemed like an unlikely match for Jett Lawson. Just like Carter and I had seemed a bit like an odd couple. But they were clearly in love, and incredibly happy.

"I'd love that," she said as she looked back at me. "Now tell me about your career. I'm just a pastry chef."

I laughed for the first time that night. "I'm not sure if I can be friends with somebody who makes pastries. You're dangerous. I love sweets, but they don't love my ass."

"I have to watch it," she said, commiserating with me. "I like to taste my own stuff. I made the cake."

"I saw it. It's spectacular," I complimented her. "And I'm having a piece whether it's on my healthy diet routine or not."

"Here comes Carter," she said enthusiastically. "I think he's missing you. He's looked over here about a hundred times. Come see me before you leave. We can chat when you have time. I can put you to work with me if you want to help at the shelters, and I want one of those bags."

I nodded automatically, and then turned to see that Carter was already beside me.

"You okay?" he asked.

"I'm fine. Ruby and I were just chatting."

He folded his arms. "You tell her everything, Ruby?"

"Only the good stuff," she shot back.

"I need to go taste that cake. You did a great job," Carter told Ruby.

"Thanks. Let me know what you think," the younger woman requested, grinning as her fiancé reached her side.

"You've never baked a pastry that I can stay away from," Carter told her as he took my hand and pulled me to my feet.

He didn't let go of my hand as he led me to the pastry table. Not only had Ruby done a cake, but every single pastry laid out on the massive buffet.

"What do you suggest?" I asked Carter politely.

"Since I know you'll only do one, I'd go for the cake." He cut a piece, put it on a plate, and handed it to me.

I tossed back the rest of the champagne in my hand and gave it to a passing waiter.

"Let's go outside," he said beside my ear. "It should be quieter there."

He grabbed my hand and pulled me along behind him.

Chapter 24

Carter

S omething was wrong with Brynn, but for the life of me, I couldn't figure out exactly what was bothering her.

From the moment I'd picked her up, she had been careful and polite.

Not the woman I knew who cracked jokes, and the female who could seem to find something amusing in almost any situation.

She'd hardly spoken on the way here, and she'd only given me one-word responses for the entire car ride.

Maybe it was her meeting. Maybe it hadn't worked out that well. But her chilly demeanor seemed to be directly related to me.

"What's wrong?" I asked her as we stepped onto the large patio of Jett's penthouse.

I took up a corner that was deserted. There were only a few other people outside because it was unseasonably chilly.

"Nothing," she denied. "I'm fine."

I watched her take a few bites of her cake, and then she set it down on the table beside us.

"Bullshit! You've been quiet all night, and being silent isn't exactly like you. You've drunk way more glasses of alcohol than you usually do, too. Something's up, and I want to know why you seem so sad. I don't like it. Did the meeting not go well?"

"On the contrary," she said. "It went really well. They want to buy the entire line, and they're offering to give me creative control. Nothing would be released without my approval."

"Did you agree?"

She shook her head. "Not yet."

"Do you want to talk about it?"

"Not really," she answered coolly.

I'd wolfed down my own cake, and set my empty plate beside hers. "Then let's talk about why you're not acting like yourself."

"Okay," she agreed. "I think maybe we should back off just a little on our relationship. It's been too much, too fast for me, Carter. I think we should take a break."

I looked at her, completely dumbfounded. "What? Are you serious?"

Jesus Christ! There was no stepping back with her for me. It was full speed ahead with every damn engine running, and it wasn't speedy enough to satisfy me.

I thought about her about fifty times a day, and when I wasn't thinking about her, I was with her.

She put a light hand on my upper arm. "I think it's all happened too fast. You have your career, and I'm leaving in a few days to go do a shoot and a commercial in California. Maybe it's our chance to step back and evaluate what kind of relationship we have. If nothing else, maybe we could be friends."

I saw red, and the hue didn't get any lighter or prettier the longer I contemplated her words. "What the fuck, Brynn? What happened between the time I saw you last night and tonight? You didn't feel this way yesterday. I know you didn't."

She looked away. "I've been thinking about it."

Mine. This woman was fucking mine, and I was not about to let her walk out of my life.

Problem was, I wanted her to be happy, too, even if it would fucking kill me to let her go.

"You can't tell me that you don't want me, Brynn. I don't fucking believe it." I took her shoulders and shook her lightly—like that would suddenly bring back the Brynn I knew.

"Lust can't keep two people together, Carter," she said in a reasonable voice that made me want to smash my fist into a wall.

"This hasn't just been lust, and you know it. You can leave if you want to, but you'll break my goddamn heart. I love you, Brynn. I think I have since the minute you told me off over the elevator incident. I was an asshole, but you changed me. You fucking healed me. Everything was black and white in my life until you came and made me see that there was color in everything. You made me see life as it really is. And nothing will ever be the same if you walk out," I said with a growl. "*You'd* be leaving *me*. Not the other way around. I thought we trusted each other. I can't be your friend, Brynn. It's not possible."

I'd sooner get dumped than try to pretend that I don't fucking need her so much that I can barely breathe because of it.

I almost caved when I saw a tear hit her cheek.

"We did trust each other," she said in a distressed tone. "But I'm just not so sure of anything anymore."

"Are you drunk?" I asked roughly, trying to jump at any excuse as to why she'd suddenly changed.

"No," she answered flatly, but the tears continued to leak from her eyes. "I'm sorry. I have to go. I'll grab a cab."

"Take the car," I demanded in a graveled voice.

Hell, even if she was dumping me, I wanted her ass to be safe.

I followed her inside, and watched as she weaved her way through the crowd and to the door.

Ever the good guest, she stopped to quickly say good-bye to Jett and Ruby before she hightailed it out the door.

I ducked back outside. I wasn't in any mood to face the party, which was starting to wind down. I found a chair in the quiet corner and sat down, still too stunned to put my thoughts together.

I wasn't sure how long I sat there before I realized that one of the couples on the balcony was actually Mason and Laura, but I turned my back on them and stared across to the Space Needle that was prominently on display.

"I think you need this," Jett said as he came and plopped his ass down beside me.

I took the generous glass of whiskey he was holding out and downed half of it in one gulp.

"What happened? Ruby thought that Brynn had been crying," Jett said.

"I have no fucking idea," I told him honestly. "Yesterday, we were fine. And today she wants to step back and look at our relationship, which pretty much means that it's over. She said we can be 'friends,' for God's sake. I can't be her goddamn *friend*. I can't keep my hands off her, and I don't want to. She. Belongs. With. Me."

"Any idea what brought all this on?" Jett questioned.

"There was nothing. No disagreement. No fight. Just the good-bye." I chugged back the rest of my drink, hoping to hell something would ease the pain.

"So that's it?" Jett asked in a somber tone.

"Hell, no, that's not it. Would you have let Ruby go that easily?" I grumbled. "I'll give her some space tonight, but I'm not going anywhere. I promised her I wouldn't, and I'm not. Something happened, Jett. And I'll figure out what it is. Brynn is it for me, man. There isn't going to be anybody else. I love her."

"I would follow Ruby through hell if she had to go there," Jett said in a grim, serious tone. "I had a feeling you weren't going to just write the whole thing off."

"I'm not. But I have to admit that I don't know what the fuck to do."

"I think you're right. Give her a little space, but not too much."

"She's getting tonight. I'll be back at her door tomorrow. She's leaving in a few days for work. We're going to work this out before she goes. If we don't, I'm going to fucking lose it."

"Go home and get some sleep. The party is over," Jett advised.

"I didn't mean to be a damper on the festivities," I told him.

"You're my brother, Carter. If you need me, I'm here for you. It doesn't matter what the circumstances are at the time."

I slapped him on the back as we stood up. "Glad your women troubles are over."

Jett shook his head and shot me a cheeky ass grin. "I hate to break it to you, but women are...complicated. You'll fight. But the make-up sex is worth it."

"I'd rather skip the fight and have regular sex," I grumbled as I followed him inside.

I *was* going to take my ornery ass home, but I already knew there would be no rest for me tonight.

Chapter 25

Laura

I knew I'd had way too much champagne and cake, but I wasn't quite sure what order I'd had them in.

My stomach was slightly upset, and I'd stepped out to get some air, totally oblivious of anybody else on the patio.

Breathe in.

Breathe out.

Breathe in.

Breathe out.

"What in the hell are you doing?" a deep, gravelly voice asked from the corner of the balcony.

"Breathing," I answered as he approached me and stopped beside me as I stared at the lights of the city.

I looked at *the voice* since watching all those fuzzy lights were making me slightly dizzy.

I was startled to see that the man beside me was Mason Lawson, the man I'd lusted after at the charity benefit where Brynn had first seen Carter.

He looked just as yummy as he had that night.

"We breathe all the time," he grumbled. "I don't think you really need to try. And you were doing it pretty loud."

"Did I disturb you?"

"No."

"Am I bothering you?"

"No."

"Then why do you want me to stop?" I knew I sounded like a total idiot, but in my alcohol-covered brain, it didn't matter.

"I just asked why you were breathing so hard."

"I ate too much cake, and drank too much champagne. That almost never happens to me."

"Then why did it happen tonight?" he questioned, sounding displeased.

Or maybe Mason was *always* displeased. It wasn't like I knew his normal demeanor.

It was a good question. Why *had* I drunk too much, and binged on cake? Now that I thought about it, I was pretty sure I'd scarfed down some of the pastries, too.

"I think I was trying to escape my own thoughts," I confessed because I didn't give a damn what I said to who at the moment.

"What were you thinking about?" he asked, like he was interrogating a witness to a crime.

"I want to have a baby," I happily admitted to him. "I'm getting old, and nobody really wants me *and* a baby. Well, I'm sure *somebody* would marry me because I'm a supermodel. Okay, I'm a *plus size* model, but I have money. Sometimes, when you make a lot of money, you're never sure why a guy wants to be with you. Do you know what I mean? And the right guy has never wanted to be with me." I was rambling, but I couldn't seem to shut up.

He let out a bark of laughter that sounded like it was rusty, and that he didn't do it much.

"How old are you?" he demanded to know.

"Thirty-three. My biological clock is ticking, and I want to be young enough to still play with my kids. If I have *kids*. Plural. Although I'd be really happy if I had one. But being an only child is lonely." Nobody knew that better than me.

"So how do you have a child if you don't have a man in your life?" he asked, sounding confused.

I slapped him on the arm. "Women don't need men anymore, silly. Well, not the *actual* man. But we do need a sperm donor. So I guess we kind of still need them. But I don't have to put up with one all the time. I just need his sperm."

"Are you trying to say that you want to have a test-tube baby?" he asked gruffly.

I nodded so hard that I made myself dizzy. "Yep. My egg, his sperm, and I'd never even have to meet the guy. I think it's better that way."

"Has it ever occurred to you that someday, that child is going to want to know something about his father?" His expression was grim.

"I'd love him or her enough to make up for the child not having two parents," I argued.

But yeah, I *had* thought about that, and *that* was probably the reason I'd cut loose and tried to forget about it at this party.

"You have time. You're beautiful and successful. You'll find somebody to do it the normal way," he said, his voice icy.

"Are you always this grumpy?" I asked.

"Are you always this chatty?" he shot back.

"As a matter of fact, I'm not. I think I'm just drunk. I guess I'd better get home."

"Do you know where it is?" he asked dryly.

"Of course I do. And you don't have to be so mean to me just because I want to have a kid. Women are doing it every day."

"I thought I was being nice," he said hesitantly. "I'm talking to you."

If he thinks he's being nice, I'd hate to see what his crabby moods are like.

"Well, thanks for the chat then," I said as I started to turn around to find my way back inside.

"Wait!" he commanded as he grabbed my arm. "I really wasn't trying to be mean."

I turned back to him. "It's okay. You don't know me, and I probably sound like a crazy drunk lady."

"Are you really trying to have a child?" He grilled me as hard as he had a moment before.

"I am. I've always wanted to have a family." I felt the tears well up in my eyes, but because I was hammered, I didn't even try to control them.

He put his enormous hands on my shoulders. "You'll find somebody. You can give it some more time. Hell, I'm thirty-four and I haven't even thought about having kids. Or a wife, for that matter."

"You're a man. You can father kids until you die. I can't. My clock is ticking."

"It's not ticking that damn loud," he snapped.

I was beginning to think that Mason Lawson had no idea how to be nice. But he was listening.

God, he was a handsome devil. His hair was dark, but his eyes were a smoldering gray, which I found pretty damn sexy.

"It is loud." My words came out terribly slurred. "Loud enough that I'm considering going to a sperm bank. I turn thirty-four in a couple of months."

"Have you ever considered using somebody you know? Somebody who can at least give you a medical history and a background? A guy who the kid can visit when he comes of age?" His voice was still chilly, and his eyes were focused directly on my face.

"Oh, God no. I don't know any man who'd be willing to do that."

"I might know one," he rasped.

"Who?"

I wanted desperately to hear his answer, and I was pretty sure that he actually uttered *Me* before I passed out in his arms and he caught me before I hit the ground.

Chapter 26

Brynn

I didn't know how to feel after I got back to my condo. I wished I could stay numb. It was safer that way. But every word Carter had said was tearing at my heart.

Yesterday, I would have been weeping in joy because he said he loved me. Now, I was bawling my eyes out because he'd said those words, but I definitely wasn't, in any way, ecstatic.

I got out of my little black dress, slipped into a pair of boy shorts and a cropped t-shirt that I slept in, and made myself some coffee.

Carter was right about one thing...I'd consumed a lot more alcohol than I normally would. And I knew why. I was trying to escape.

I hated myself for that.

My plan had been to get through the party, and then give him a chance to explain. Not that there actually was an explanation for him being that close to another female, but I'd owed it to him to at least have the chance to say *something*.

Instead, I'd simply pushed him away because it was way easier than opening myself up to get slammed.

I sipped my coffee at the small kitchen table, thinking about every single time he'd reassured me, only to end up cheating on me in the end.

Maybe he hadn't slept with the female yet, but it didn't matter. Emotional cheating was just as bad as physically fucking another woman. Maybe worse.

I was getting my brain back now that I was filling up with caffeine, and it had been awhile since my last drink.

I hadn't been drunk, but the alcohol had been enough to make me shy away from anything raw. It had opened the door for the emotions to rush through, and all I wanted to do was close the damn thing.

I wanted to call my mother just to see how she was doing, but it was after midnight, three a.m. her time, so I'd have to wait until tomorrow.

After hearing about the hell that Ruby had been through, I guess all I really needed was to thank her for always being there, and loving me as much as she always had.

We hadn't had a lot of money, but she'd kept a roof over our heads after my father had gone to prison. And I was what I was today because of her. Well, maybe not the heartbroken part. But the independent, career-minded, wealthy woman I usually was.

The final fog lifted from my mind, and all I could feel was pain.

I should have given him a chance to say what he wanted to say.

I should have given him the opportunity to explain.

And I should have listened.

Looking back to all of the things that had been said and done between us, I should have given him that chance.

After all, Carter had essentially healed a wound that had festered inside me for years. And even though it was highly possible that he may have betrayed me, at least I knew that I was capable of trusting someone. Even if that person wasn't going to be him.

Do it, Brynn. Just do it. Rip the damn Band-Aid off and find out the truth!

In the end, I knew *me*, and I wasn't going to be able to move on until I heard the truth from his lips.

Before I could think better of it, I grabbed my purse and rummaged around inside until I found the key to his penthouse. I'd never used it, but I was glad I had it.

I swiped my own keys from the table, and headed upstairs.

I have to know the truth. I have to know the truth.

When I finally got to the door of his home, I hesitated briefly, but then gathered my courage and rang the doorbell.

He answered the door almost immediately, and my heart sunk when I saw the ravaged look on his face.

His tie was unknotted and hanging around his neck, and his tux looked like he'd slept in it.

I swallowed hard. "You said if I ever needed you, I could just come up. Can I come in?"

His gaze was cool, but he swung the door open and I stepped inside.

"I have to ask you a question, and I really hope you can be honest with me," I began.

His stare went to my attire. I'd forgotten I was dressed for bed. I'd been too intent on getting the answers to my questions.

"I've always been honest with you, Brynn," he answered in a flat tone.

"You told me you had a meeting yesterday, but when I left the café I'd had my meeting in, I saw you. I saw you at the jewelry store with another woman, Carter. I saw you hug her, and I saw you kiss her. You weren't at a meeting. You were with another woman," I said.

He looked puzzled for a second, and then his expression became completely shuttered.

Without a word, he turned and headed toward the bedroom. He was back within a minute.

"You're right," he said distantly, like he was having a casual conversation. "I wasn't at a meeting. That was my one and only little white lie, and I probably justified it because I wanted Harper to help me pick this out."

I audibly gasped as he pulled a jewelry box from that store out of his pocket and flipped it open. Nestled in the red velvet lining was the most exquisite diamond I'd ever seen.

The setting was either platinum or white gold, and it had a huge center stone that sparkled and winked, even in the dimly lit room. The big diamond was flanked by two smaller ones set back so that it didn't detract from the gorgeous middle stone.

"Oh, my God," I said, horrified. "That was Harper in the store with you."

"Of course," he said offhandedly. "And if I did kiss her, it was brotherly and not romantic. I hadn't seen her in a while, and I was happy that she was with me. I made her promise to keep quiet about it until I had the right spot to propose. I wanted to marry you, Brynn. I loved you."

The fact that he was using past tense was a little scary.

Shit! What in the hell had I done? "I couldn't really see her. I just saw you put your arm around her and kiss the top of her head like you always do with me. I'm so sorry, Carter." My heart was splintering into a million little pieces.

I'd hurt him. I could see the devastation on his face.

"It never occurred to you that there could be a logical explanation?" he asked in a clipped voice. "Granted, I never should have lied about the meeting, but I didn't want you to find out. But you tossed our relationship away over something pretty damn petty." He closed the box and shoved it back into his pocket.

"I love you, too, Carter. I really do. I just got scared. It was like the worst thing I could imagine happening had come true."

There was silence as his frosty gaze bore into me.

Finally, I asked hesitantly, "You don't want to give me the ring anymore?"

Pain sliced through my soul as I saw the doubtful look on his face. He didn't want to marry me.

I'd killed the fragile love that had grown between the two of us.

He raked a hand through his hair. "Christ! I don't know what I want anymore. Earlier, I swore I was going to give you some time, and that I'd be here when you were ready. I even planned on dogging you until you told me what the hell had happened. But now, knowing such a ridiculous thing sent you off without even talking to me, or better yet, you just coming into the store when you saw me, makes me wonder if you'll just keep running. Or if you're just making excuses to run because that's really what you want. I don't think I can deal with that, Brynn. You didn't even give me a chance to tell you the real truth."

I tried to blink back the tears that filled my eyes, but it was a useless battle. He was right, and he had every right to be angry.

"I was going to talk to you after the party. But you're right, I drank too much, and I didn't know how to handle it."

He was quiet, his expression still turbulent.

"I don't blame you for being hesitant," I said in a quivering voice. "I was stupid. I went with a knee-jerk reaction, and let it take over every one of my thoughts."

Carter had wanted to marry me.

He'd loved me *that much*.

And I'd tossed it away. I'd tossed *him* away.

"I really don't know what to do right now, Brynn."

I swiped at the river of tears that were flowing down my face. "I understand," I choked out. "But I want you to know that I love you. I think I have since you kissed me in that elevator. You've done so much for me, and I hate myself that I doubted you, even for a second."

"You changed my life, too," he said in a slightly warmer voice. "But I need more. I get that couples fight, and I'd fight with you any damn day of the week. I just can't take it that you might run at the first sign of trouble."

My heart was aching, and all I wanted to do was throw myself into his arms and beg for forgiveness until he gave it to me.

But he was wary now, and he wasn't going to give me a second chance.

"I know," I agreed tearfully. "I broke the bond of trust we had. It's my fault."

I'd lost the best thing that had ever happened to me in my life, and it was all because I let myself give in to my fear.

"Maybe we should talk about it when we've both had time to think," he suggested flatly.

I knew what that meant. He wasn't going to be able to forget that he'd given me everything he had, and I'd hurt him irrevocably.

"It's okay," I told him wistfully. "I'll go."

He didn't protest as I opened the door and let it close behind me. Not that I'd expected him to.

I got into the elevator and rode it back down to my floor, thinking about the fact that I wasn't going to lose Carter because he'd betrayed me. I was going to lose him because I hadn't completely shaken off my insecurities.

I couldn't go back in time and change what I'd done, but I was going to put myself out there completely to Carter. I wasn't giving up until I was convinced there was no chance for us at all.

Maybe I didn't deserve a second chance. But I wasn't letting go of Carter without a fight.

Chapter 27

Brynn

"How is it that I didn't sleep much last night, but you look worse than I do?" I asked Laura early the next morning as I took a seat across from her at the diner where we were meeting up.

I'd gotten an email from my agent asking if I could get a flight out the next morning for California. My client wanted to start the shoot and commercial early, so I'd booked a flight last night.

Then, Laura had called early, and we'd decided to meet up for coffee before I had to get to the airport.

My bag was in my car, and I had about an hour to spare.

I assessed Laura's face, and I wasn't liking what I saw. The bags under her eyes were dark, like she hadn't slept much at all. And her expression was stressed. She had her fingers around the coffee mug like it was her only savior.

"What's wrong?" I pressed. "Is everything okay?"

She planted her face in her hand. "No. Oh, my God, Brynn, I drank way too much last night."

"Not like we haven't done that before," I reminded her.

"But I didn't know anyone at the party. I feel like an idiot," she said with a moan. "At my worst, I was talking to Mason Lawson. Honestly, I don't remember what all I said, but I remember telling him that I wanted to have a baby."

I knew Laura was a private person, but... "What's wrong with that? It's true."

"I think he offered to be the baby daddy for me. Everything is vague. Maybe I'm wrong, but I swear he said he'd be willing to do it."

I whistled. "I can think of way worse sperm donors."

"I'm mortified here, buddy. From what I remember, I was a twit. He must think I'm a total idiot. Not that it matters because I'm not likely to run into him again. So if I can just stop thinking about what he thought, I'd be good."

"He's just one guy, Laura. Really, who cares what he thinks?"

She sat up straight again, but her face was still haggard. "You're right. It just seems a tiny bit mortifying that I suddenly became chatty with one of the richest guys on the planet."

"What else did you talk about?" I asked curiously.

"Nothing I can remember, thank God. It was a short conversation. Thanks for getting me back home."

"Laura, I didn't take you home." She must have been really out of it.

She looked at me in horror. "But I was home in my bed this morning. How in the hell did I get there? My car was still at Jett's place. I had to go pick it up this morning. Damn, I've never forgotten how I got home."

"Laura, what's wrong? I've never seen you get that trashed." Although I was glad she got home safe, I was worried about what had caused her to lose it in the first place.

She shrugged. "I started the search for a possible sperm donor. It all seemed so...cold. Do you know that you have to actually shop for a donor? They take MasterCard, Visa, Discover, and American Express. It's not like I'm ordering a pizza or something. It's a baby, for God's sake. I started thinking about how I was going to tell my child someday that I ordered him or her like I was buying a new computer.

And I have no idea what traits I want. Education level, medical history, ethnicity, physical characteristics, personality traits—blah, blah, blah. And what if my kid ends up with biological siblings? Do I want the donor open to seeing my baby some day?"

"I didn't know you'd gotten that far into it," I said, a little hurt that Laura hadn't shared that with me earlier.

"I wasn't really. I just went for a consult. But they asked me to start looking for a donor if I was interested."

"So it's more complicated than you thought?" I questioned.

"Actually, I think it was far too easy. I pick a guy who has all the traits I want, go to the checkout, and I'm done. The process isn't complicated at all. But all I can think about is how all this works out in the future. I guess that's why I just wanted to let go for a while last night. But I went way too far," she said with a weary sigh.

"Please don't let this stress you out," I said softly. "You don't have to go through with it, and you have time to think about it. Unless you made a purchase. And even then, nobody is going to force you."

She shook her head. "I didn't. I guess I just wanted to see what the process was like. Getting pregnant isn't the problem. It's all the other things I worry about down the road."

I could definitely understand her predicament.

"Take your time," I advised. "And don't worry about what you said to Mason. From what Carter tells me, he's basically a workaholic. He'll likely forget all about it."

So much for the possible hookup between Laura and Mason. I was hoping they'd get along.

"I hope so," she mumbled. "So how did it go for you guys at the party? When I saw you, I can't say you looked especially happy."

Laura and I had been together at the party until Ruby had pulled me aside, and somebody else had wanted to chat with my best friend.

"I screwed up. I tried to break up with Carter instead of confronting him about the woman I saw him with at the jewelry store. Turns out, it was his sister, Harper, and he was buying *me* an engagement ring—with her help. Now we're broken up for good because I pushed him away," I told her, my heart aching all over again.

"Oh, Brynn. I'm so sorry. I wish you had just asked him."

I ordered a coffee, and then explained to Laura what had happened the night before.

"Did he say he didn't want to see you again?" she questioned.

"No. But I'd say he was pretty certain. I'm kind of glad that I'm flying out this morning. Maybe being somewhere else for a few weeks will help." Everything in Seattle was going to remind me of Carter, and the local media loved covering all things Lawson.

"He still loves you, Brynn. And you love him, right?" Laura asked gently.

I nodded, not trusting myself to speak without blubbering in the middle of the diner.

"Maybe you can work it out when you get back. Carter might be angry, but he isn't unreasonable. He knows about your history."

"He does. But there comes a point when I have to leave that behind. He's never given me any reason not to trust him. Just the opposite. It was a reaction that came out of nowhere, an insecurity from my past. God, he loved me so much he was going to ask me to marry him," I said a little louder than I should have.

"Believe me, he's not going to give you up. Give him time," she said.

"I'm not going to give him that much space. I love Carter. I *want* to marry him. I can't imagine being with anybody else," I told her. "I guess I'm just going to have to prove that I'm really not willing to let go. That I'm not going to run away for some idiotic reason that isn't even true ever again."

"That's the woman I know and love," Laura said with a smile. "You've never backed down. Don't start now."

"I don't plan on it." I shot her a weak grin, and then looked at the clock. "Oh, God, I have to go. I have a plane to catch."

I stood up and grabbed my purse.

"I'll get the coffee." Laura waved me on. "Just go."

"Don't make any decisions without me," I pleaded. "I want to be there if you decide to go through with the insemination."

"I won't. I really need to think about it," she agreed.

She stood, and I hugged her quickly before I rushed out of the restaurant.

When I got to my car, I pulled out my phone to shoot off a quick text. It would be one of many over the next few weeks, but if Carter wanted me to quit doing it, he'd have to tell me to my face.

If not, he'd be hearing from me every single day.

Chapter 28

Brynn

<u>Day One:</u>
Brynn: *I love you. I'm sorry.*
<u>Day Two:</u>
Brynn: *I miss you. I'm sorry.*
<u>Day Three:</u>
Brynn: *I love you. Miss you, too. I'm sorry.*
<u>Day Four:</u>
Brynn: *I'm not going anywhere. I'm sorry.*

I kept scrolling down the list of texts I'd sent Carter over the last two weeks, every one of them the same, but slightly different.

I was ready to leave California, but my heart was heavy.

My bags were packed, and I was waiting on my transport to the airport, but I still had time, so I plopped my ass on the bed of my hotel room.

He hadn't sent me a single response.

You knew this wasn't going to be easy.

I *had* known, and I was ready to get back to Seattle to resume the fight to get Carter to talk to me.

It hadn't been easy focusing on my job. It was hard to try to be radiant when I felt like crap.

And not hearing from Carter had worn me down more every day.

Was he even reading my messages anymore?

Did he care?

Or was he just…done?

I startled as my phone vibrated.

My hand started to shake as I saw who had sent a text.

Carter: It's about time you finished your work there.

I started to hyperventilate.

Brynn: How did you know I was done?

Carter: The CEO of the company is an acquaintance of mine.

I smiled. Of course he could pick up the phone and call any executive. He was Carter Lawson. But why had he wanted to do that?

I tried hard not to get my hopes too high. After all, I'd been texting him for two weeks with no answer.

Carter: There's a car downstairs to pick you up, and my jet is at the airport.

Brynn: Now?

Carter: Right fucking now. Get moving.

I wasn't about to argue about his bossiness. I was headed to the lobby in a little less than a minute with my suitcase and carry-on in tow.

He's willing to talk to me.

He sent his plane and his car.

Does that mean he wants me back in Seattle so we can rationally discuss what happened?

I stopped short as I walked out the sliding doors in the lobby, mesmerized by what was right in front of me at the curb.

I didn't much give a damn about the fancy car.

Carter leaning casually against that vehicle with a bouquet of red roses was a totally different matter.

I let go of my bags as the chauffeur came to get them and put them in the trunk, and stepped closer to Carter.

God, he looked amazing.

He was put together in a gray custom suit, and another blue tie that complemented the beautiful blue eyes that were currently unreadable.

"You're here," I simply said breathlessly.

"So I am," he replied as he held out the flowers to me.

"They're beautiful," I told him as I took them.

"*You're* beautiful," he corrected. "I could have sworn I asked you not to fly commercial."

"We broke up," I stammered.

"I never broke up. I just didn't think quick enough. Come here." He opened his arms.

I flew into them without a second thought, my heart hammering as he tightened his arms around me.

I breathed in his scent, the same masculine smell that always made me half crazy. "I love you, Carter. I love you so much. I'm so sorry. I was stupid."

"Stop!" he growled. "Just stop. I already know you're sorry. You've sent me fourteen messages about it. That's over. I don't care anymore. It was just a mistake. All I want to do is hold you right now. Jesus, Brynn. I missed you so damn much."

I started to cry, blubbering all over his expensive suit until he opened the car door and helped me get in, then slid over beside me to take me into his arms again.

But I didn't stop crying. They were tears of relief. Tears of joy. Tears of happiness that Carter wasn't going to hold my mistake against me forever. "When you didn't answer my texts, I didn't know if you were going to ever talk to me again," I choked out.

He swiped gently at the droplets on my cheeks as he said, "Don't cry. I didn't answer because if I did, it would have been in person. And I knew you had a job to do. But it fucking killed me not to. But I will now. I love you, too, Brynn Davis. Always will. No matter how many mistakes you make, or how many I make, we stay together. I have no doubt I'm going to fuck up in the future, but one thing I'll never do is be with any other woman but you."

"I should have never assumed that you were," I told him gently. "The ghosts of my past rose up to bite me. But it was never about you. It was about me. I should have stridden into that store, confident that you were with someone who wasn't a romantic interest. But I was scared. All of this has been so good, and it happened so fast. I guess I was waiting for something to go wrong when it didn't really have to."

He put two fingers on my lips. "Don't, Brynn. I know about your past, and I should have been more sympathetic. But I didn't know you were going to take off the next morning. I was at your door not long after you left, but you were already gone. By the time I finally thought about calling Laura, your plane had already taken off. I knew I was going to have to wait. But patience has never exactly been one of my virtues," he said with a grin.

I felt the car starting to move, and I lay back against him with a sigh, grateful that he'd been patient enough, even if he hadn't liked it.

Being in his arms was like coming home for me, and I didn't ever want to leave again.

"Thank you for coming to get me," I murmured.

"Did you think I wouldn't?" he asked gruffly. "Hell, I missed you every minute you were gone. I wanted to come get you the moment I found out where you were. But I would have never left again without you."

I smiled. "I do wish you would have answered me at least once. I felt kind of stupid just texting for myself."

"You weren't texting just for yourself. I waited for that damn message every day. I think it's the only thing that helped me wait another day."

"I'll try to be more secure. You've never given me any reason to doubt anything you said," I explained.

"I'll make sure you never doubt a single thing about us," he said huskily.

I turned around in his arms, wanting to see his eyes. I didn't get to see them for very long because Carter took my face in his hands and kissed me.

And I sank into his embrace, finally realizing that, no matter what, he'd never let go.

Epilogue

Brynn

One Month Later...

Things were almost perfect in my life since Carter and I had gotten back together again.

He still said that we'd never really been apart, that he'd never broken up with me, and I didn't argue with him.

But what had happened had been my wake-up call to what life would be like without him, and that fear was something I never wanted to experience again.

Not that Carter and I didn't fight. When you put two independent, hardheaded people together, it was bound to happen. But it had never gotten out of hand again.

We talked.

We listened to each other.

And we resolved our issues.

And then we had make-up sex.

The one part of the disagreements that both of us thoroughly enjoyed.

"Hello, beautiful. What are you doing out here?"

I looked up from the design I was working on to see the handsome man behind the voice.

Carter.

It was funny that my mouth still went dry every single time I looked at him. Was there ever going to be a day when my heart didn't skitter when I heard his voice?

God, I hope not.

"I wasn't expecting you quite this early." He was home from work much earlier than usual.

I was working from his penthouse, and I rarely used my condo for anything but storage anymore.

There wasn't a night that we didn't want to be together, and I loved the fact that he had an amazing patio. It was getting a little bit colder in the evenings, but it was still warm enough for me to work outside during the day.

"I missed you," he replied simply.

I rose from the lounger I was sitting on, and moved to put my arms around his neck.

He wrapped me up in a warm embrace that never failed to make me feel like I was his entire world.

"I missed you, too," I murmured, taking a deep breath of him as he held me tightly in his arms.

"Should we go out to celebrate the deal you made for your new line?" he asked in a husky tone.

I'd just signed the contract with Alicia yesterday, and I was still reeling from the amount of money they'd offered me. But the best thing about it wasn't the money. It was the freedom I'd bargained for to design and approve every new bag that went on the market.

I'd been elated, but it was really just icing on an already sweet cake.

I pulled back so I could see his face. "I'm cooking. And I picked up some of Ruby's pastries when I met her and Lia at the coffee shop today. God, they look amazing."

I'd started to meet with Ruby and her best friend, Lia, often at the coffee shop that Lia owned. Ruby was Lia's supplier for baked goods, and it was never easy to turn down one of those tempting pastries to go with my coffee fix.

"Are you actually going to eat one of them?" he asked with a grin.

"Already had one this morning, and I'll have a second one with you if you help me work off the calories later," I teased.

"Deal," he answered, so fast that it made my head spin. "But I did come home early for a reason, so don't get me distracted with fantasies about later."

I looked at him, trying to figure out from his expression if something was wrong. "Is everything okay?"

"I didn't say it was bad news," he remarked.

"Is it?"

He shook his head. "No. I'm hoping you'll think it's good."

I sighed. "Sorry. I'm still a work in progress. I guess I'm always waiting for the other shoe to drop."

My first inclination was to always assume something was going to go wrong because my relationship with Carter was so damn good, but I was working on that.

"Come inside," he urged, grabbing my hand to pull me through the sliding door, and then closing it behind him.

He reached into his pocket and pulled out a small box that looked suspiciously like…

Oh, God.

When I described my life as *almost perfect*, it was because I'd never seen the ring that Carter had bought me again, nor had he proposed.

I'd tried not to let it bother me, but it was in the back of my mind almost all the time.

"I couldn't give you the same ring, and I couldn't get it from that jewelry store," he said hoarsely. "Too many bad memories associated with both of them, so I went somewhere else to get another one that was custom designed. It took a while to get it sized and put together. But it finally came today. So I need to ask you the question I've wanted to ask you for almost two months."

He popped open the box, and I released the breath I'd been holding while he was talking.

It was a different color box, but a gorgeous ring was still sitting in the center of a red velvet interior.

And it was breathtaking.

My eyes went from the spectacular diamond to Carter's face.

My heart started galloping as I looked at the serious intent in his gorgeous eyes.

"Marry me, Brynn. Put me out of my damn misery. I love you. I'll always need you. You've made me a much better man than I was before I met you."

I finally blinked, and that released a flood of happy tears that I couldn't contain.

"Oh, Carter," I said in a breathless voice. "Yes. You know I'm going to say yes. I love you, too."

It touched my soul that he didn't want to remind me of my mistakes, and had gone to the trouble of getting me a different ring from another store. And I was glad that I hadn't let my insecurities run rampant because he hadn't produced the ring again.

I'd waited.

And everything had been explained.

My hand shook just a little as he placed the ring on my finger.

"It's gorgeous," I said with awe.

"I'm just damn glad to see my ring on your finger," he said. "You better set the date pretty quickly or we'll be making a trip to Vegas."

I hugged him, and he picked me up and twirled me around.

I laughed, even though I still had tears trickling down my cheeks. "I wouldn't mind a quiet wedding like that."

"Your mother wouldn't be happy," he warned.

"She probably wouldn't," I conceded. "I'm her only child."

"I can wait," he said in a voice that didn't sound like he wanted to wait at all. "But make it soon. I've waited long enough for you."

I looked at him, knowing my heart was in my eyes, but I wasn't the tiniest bit concerned. Carter met my gaze with his own open expression.

He lifted his hand and tenderly wiped the tears from my face. "Don't cry. I told you this was something good."

B. A. Scott

"Kiss me," I requested, unable to wait any longer to be connected with him in some way.

He bent his head and covered my mouth with his, and that embrace was a promise of all the things that Carter and I would experience together in the future.

He was wrong about our engagement being *something good*.

It was more than *good*.

Carter was mine, and I was his.

My life was now *absolutely perfect*.

~The End~

Please visit me at:
http://www.authorjsscott.com
http://www.facebook.com/authorjsscott

You can write to me at
jsscott_author@hotmail.com

You can also tweet
@AuthorJSScott

Please sign up for my Newsletter for updates,
new releases and exclusive excerpts.

Books by J. S. Scott:

The Billionaire's Obsession Series:
The Billionaire's Obsession
Heart of The Billionaire
The Billionaire's Salvation
The Billionaire's Game
Billionaire Undone
Billionaire Unmasked
Billionaire Untamed
Billionaire Unbound
Billionaire Undaunted
Billionaire Unknown
Billionaire Unveiled

Billionaire Unloved
Billionaire Unchallenged
Billionaire Unattainable

The Sinclairs:
The Billionaire's Christmas
No Ordinary Billionaire
The Forbidden Billionaire
The Billionaire's Touch
The Billionaire's Voice
The Billionaire Takes All
The Billionaire's Secrets
Only a Millionaire

The Accidental Billionaires
Ensnared

The Walker Brothers:
Release!
Player!
Damaged!

A Dark Horse Novel:
Bound
Hacked

.